FAR OUT
FAIRY TALES

STONE ARCH BOOKS
a capstone imprint

INTRODUCING...

TEAM MAYHEM MICE

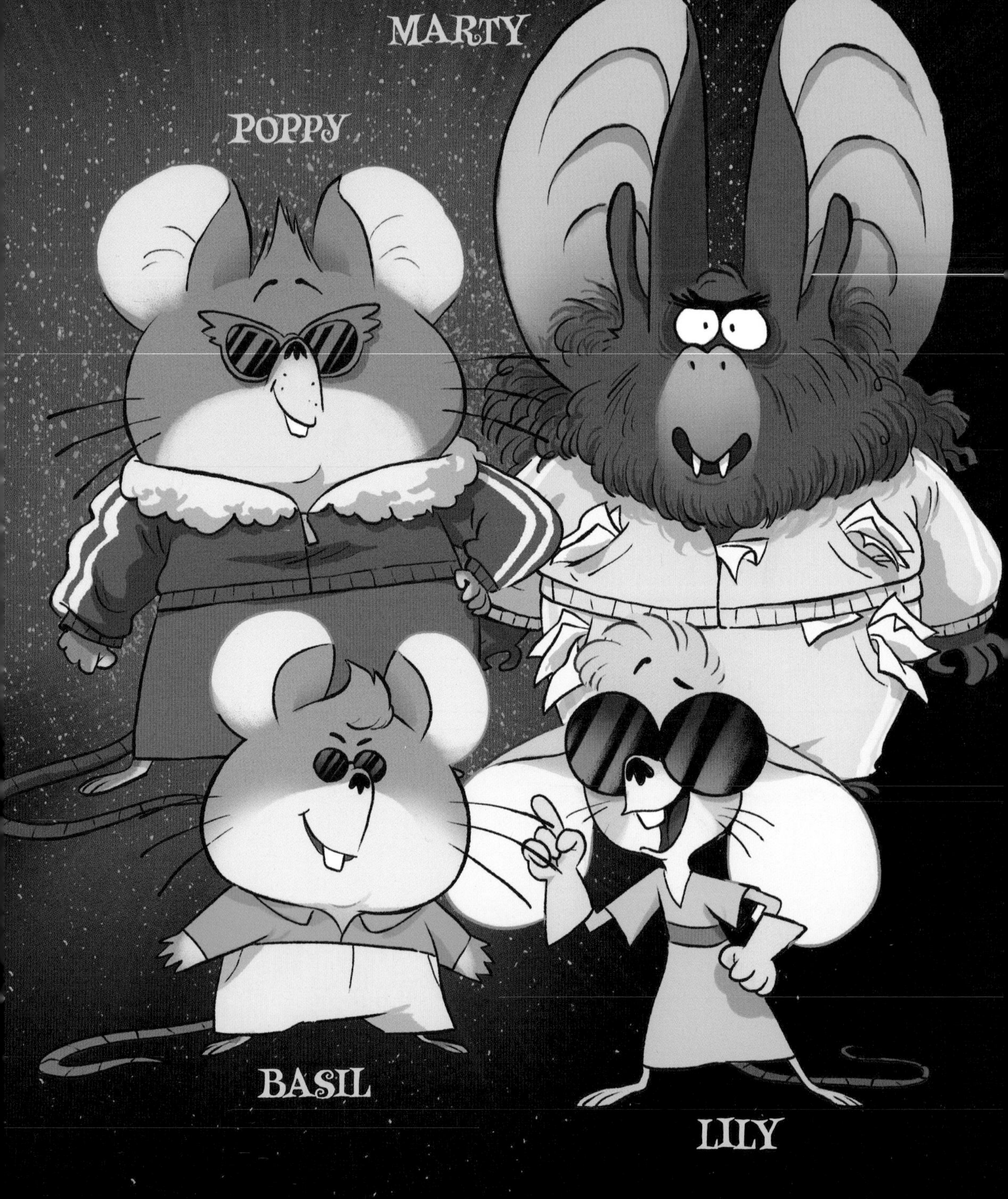
MARTY
POPPY
BASIL
LILY

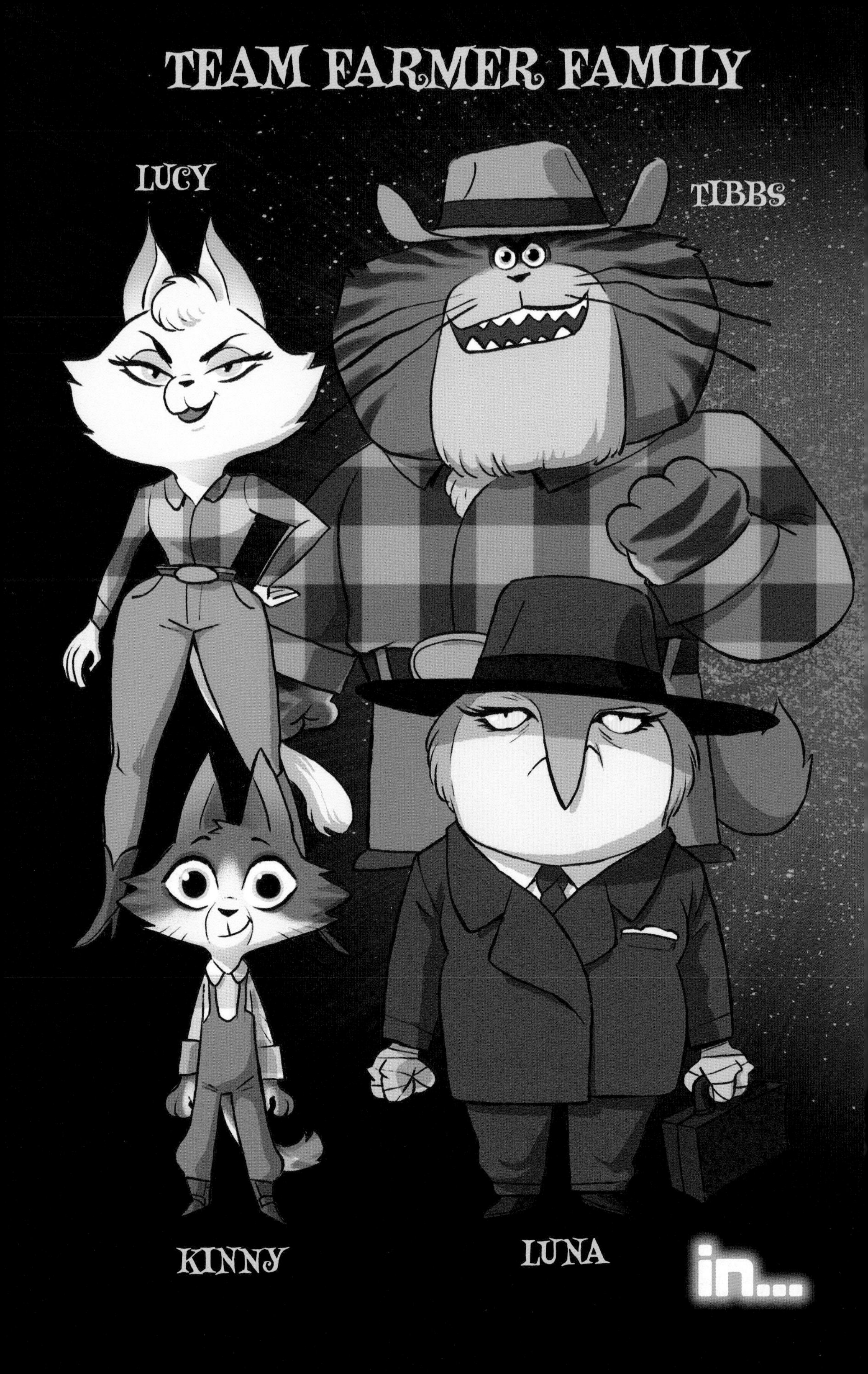
TEAM FARMER FAMILY
LUCY
TIBBS
KINNY
LUNA
in...

Published by Stone Arch Books,
an imprint of Capstone.
1710 Roe Crest Drive
North Mankato, Minnesota 56003
capstonepub.com

Library of Congress Cataloging-in-
Publication Data
Names: Walls, Jasmine, author. |
Cantero, Jonatan, illustrator.
Title: Three blind mice race for
revenge : a graphic novel / by Jasmine
Walls ; illustrated by Jonatan Cantero.
Other titles: Far out fairy tales.
Description: North Mankato,
Minnesota : Stone Arch Books,
an imprint of Capstone, 2023. |
Series: Far out fairy tales | Audience:
Ages 8-11 | Audience: Grades 4-6 |
Summary: It is time for the Golden
Chalice Race, and the three blind mice
Poppy, Basil, and Lily are competing
using sonar tech to navigate the
twisting track; but the Farmer Family
cats are determined to win and
have plans to sabotage the Mayhem
Mice—just as they did in the last race,
cutting off the tails of the mice's
vehicles.
Identifiers: LCCN 2022004740 (print)
| LCCN 2022004741 (ebook) |
ISBN 9781666335583 (hardcover) |
ISBN 9781666335521 (paperback) |
ISBN 9781666335538 (pdf) | ISBN
9781666335552 (kindle edition)
Subjects: LCSH: Three blind mice—
Adaptations. | Nursery rhymes—
Adaptations. | Mice—Juvenile fiction.
| Racing—Juvenile fiction. | CYAC:
Characters in literature—Fiction.
| Mice—Fiction. | Races—Fiction. |
Graphic novels. | LCGFT: Graphic
novels. | Nursery rhymes. | Graphic
novel adaptations.
Classification: LCC PZ7.7.W358
Thr 2022 (print) | LCC PZ7.7.W358
(ebook) | DDC 741.5/973—dc23/
eng/20220201
LC record available at
https://lccn.loc.gov/2022004740
LC ebook record available at
https://lccn.loc.gov/2022004741

Designed by Hilary Wacholz
Edited by Abby Huff
Colors by Mado Peña
Lettering by Jaymes Reed

FAR OUT FAIRY TALES

THREE BLIND MICE RACE FOR REVENGE

A GRAPHIC NOVEL

WRITTEN BY JASMINE WALLS

ILLUSTRATED BY JONATAN CANTERO

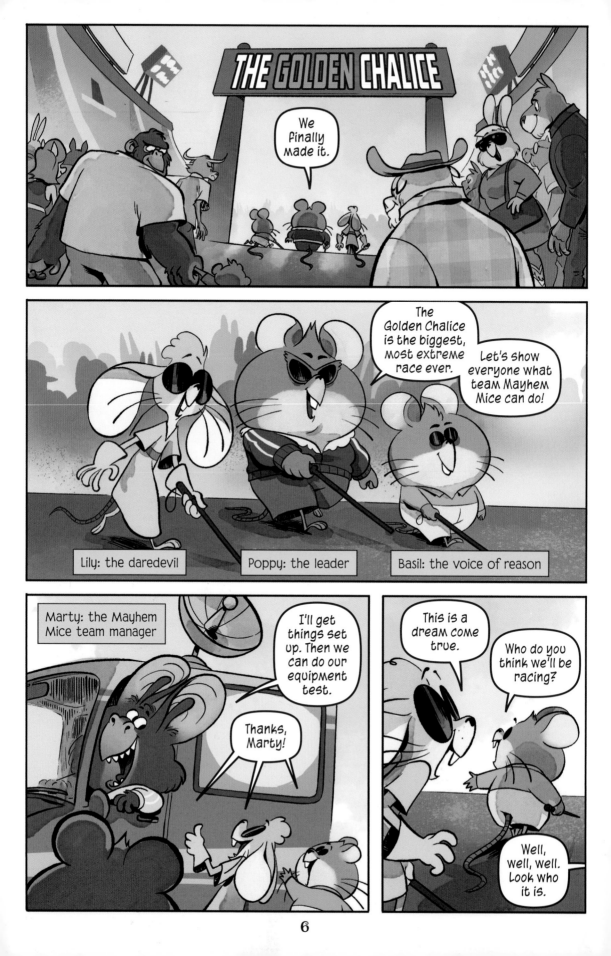

THE GOLDEN CHALICE

We finally made it.

The Golden Chalice is the biggest, most extreme race ever.

Let's show everyone what team Mayhem Mice can do!

Lily: the daredevil

Poppy: the leader

Basil: the voice of reason

Marty: the Mayhem Mice team manager

I'll get things set up. Then we can do our equipment test.

Thanks, Marty!

This is a dream come true.

Who do you think we'll be racing?

Well, well, well. Look who it is.

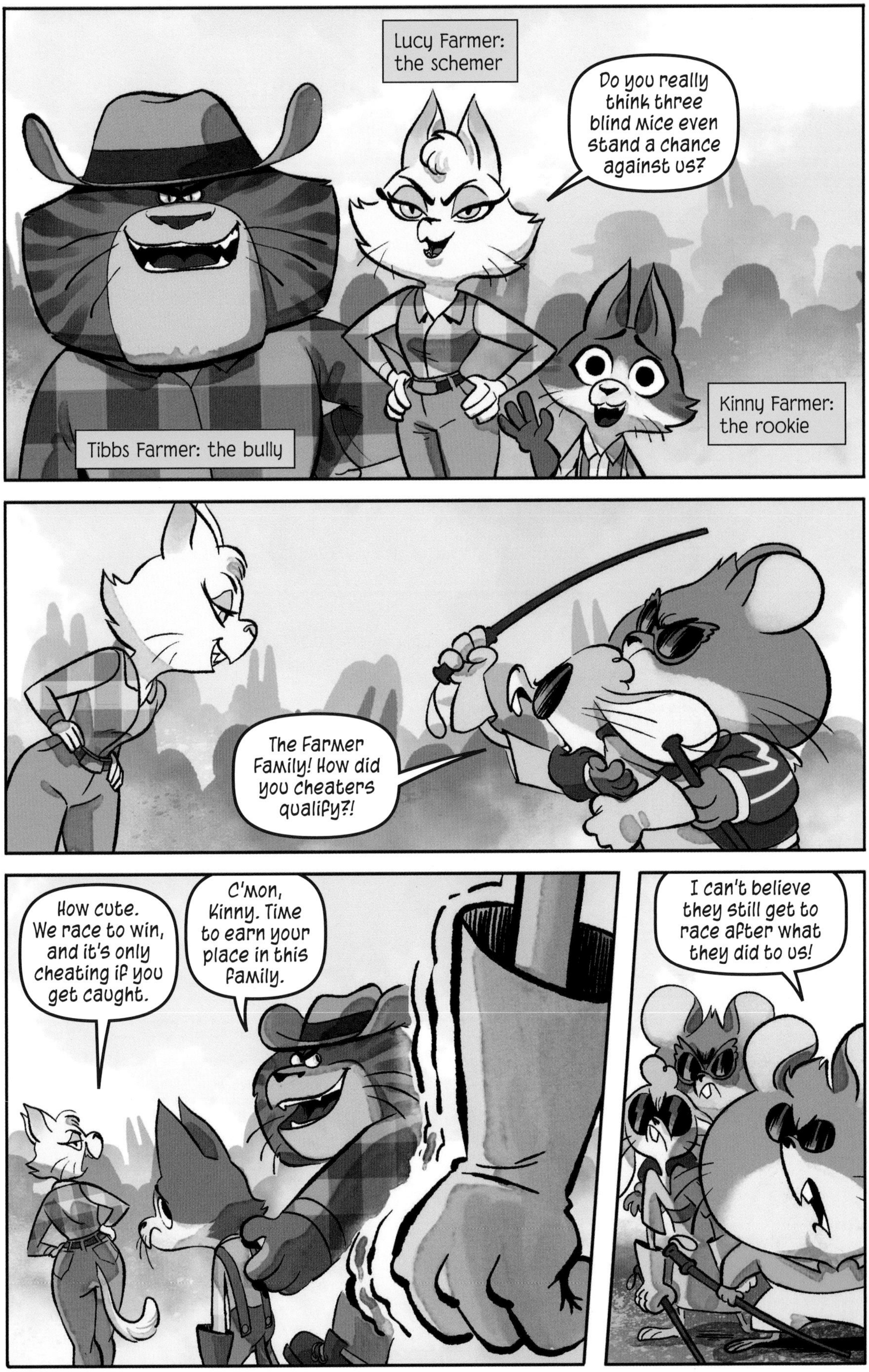
Lucy Farmer: the schemer
Do you really think three blind mice even stand a chance against us?
Tibbs Farmer: the bully
Kinny Farmer: the rookie
The Farmer Family! How did you cheaters qualify?!
How cute. We race to win, and it's only cheating if you get caught.
C'mon, Kinny. Time to earn your place in this family.
I can't believe they still get to race after what they did to us!

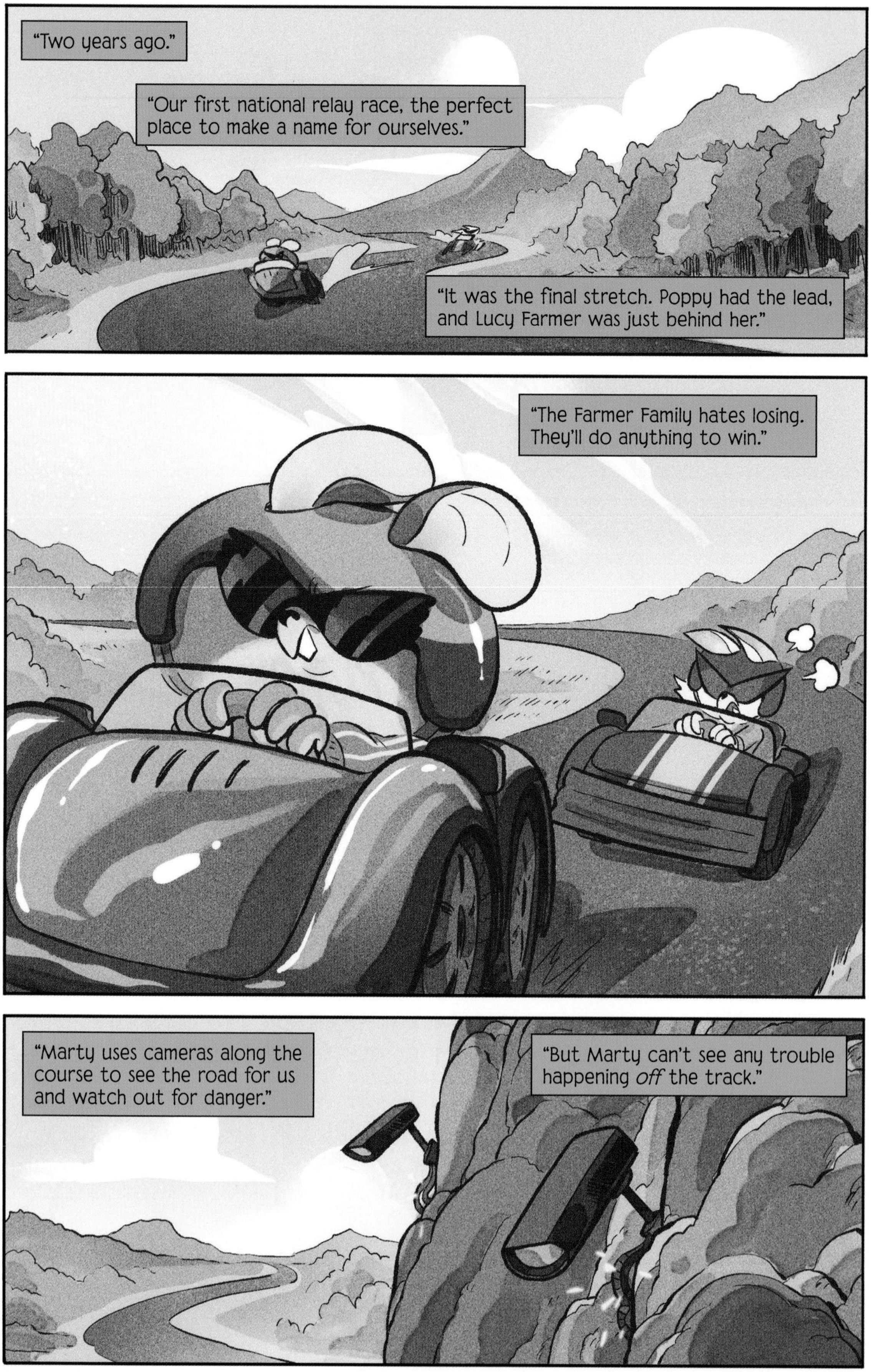
"Two years ago."
"Our first national relay race, the perfect place to make a name for ourselves."
"It was the final stretch. Poppy had the lead, and Lucy Farmer was just behind her."
"The Farmer Family hates losing. They'll do anything to win."
"Marty uses cameras along the course to see the road for us and watch out for danger."
"But Marty can't see any trouble happening *off* the track."

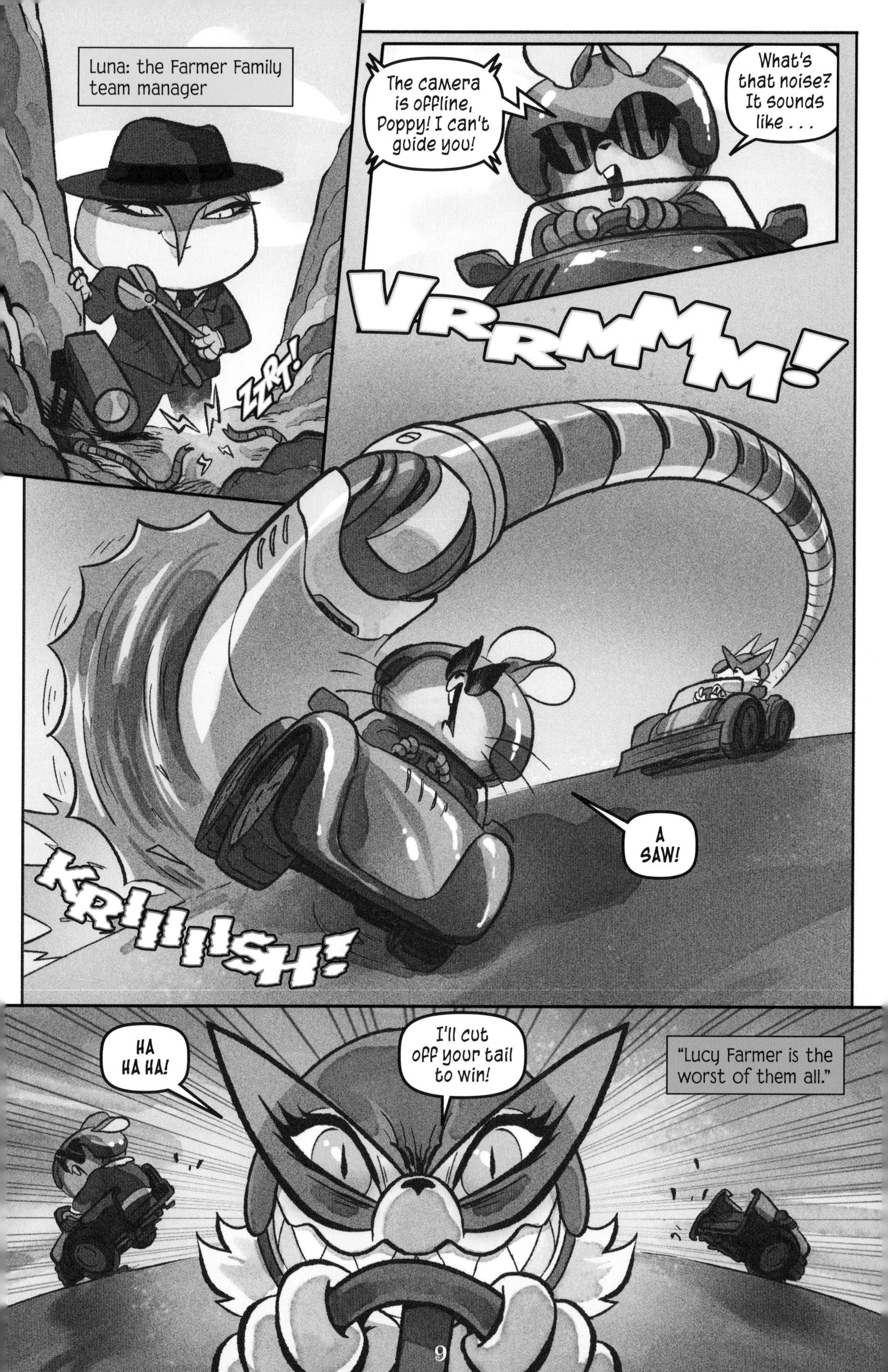
Luna: the Farmer Family team manager
ZZRT!
The camera is offline, Poppy! I can't guide you!
What's that noise? It sounds like . . .
VRRMMMM!
A SAW!
KRIIIIISH!
HA HA HA!
I'll cut off your tail to win!
"Lucy Farmer is the worst of them all."

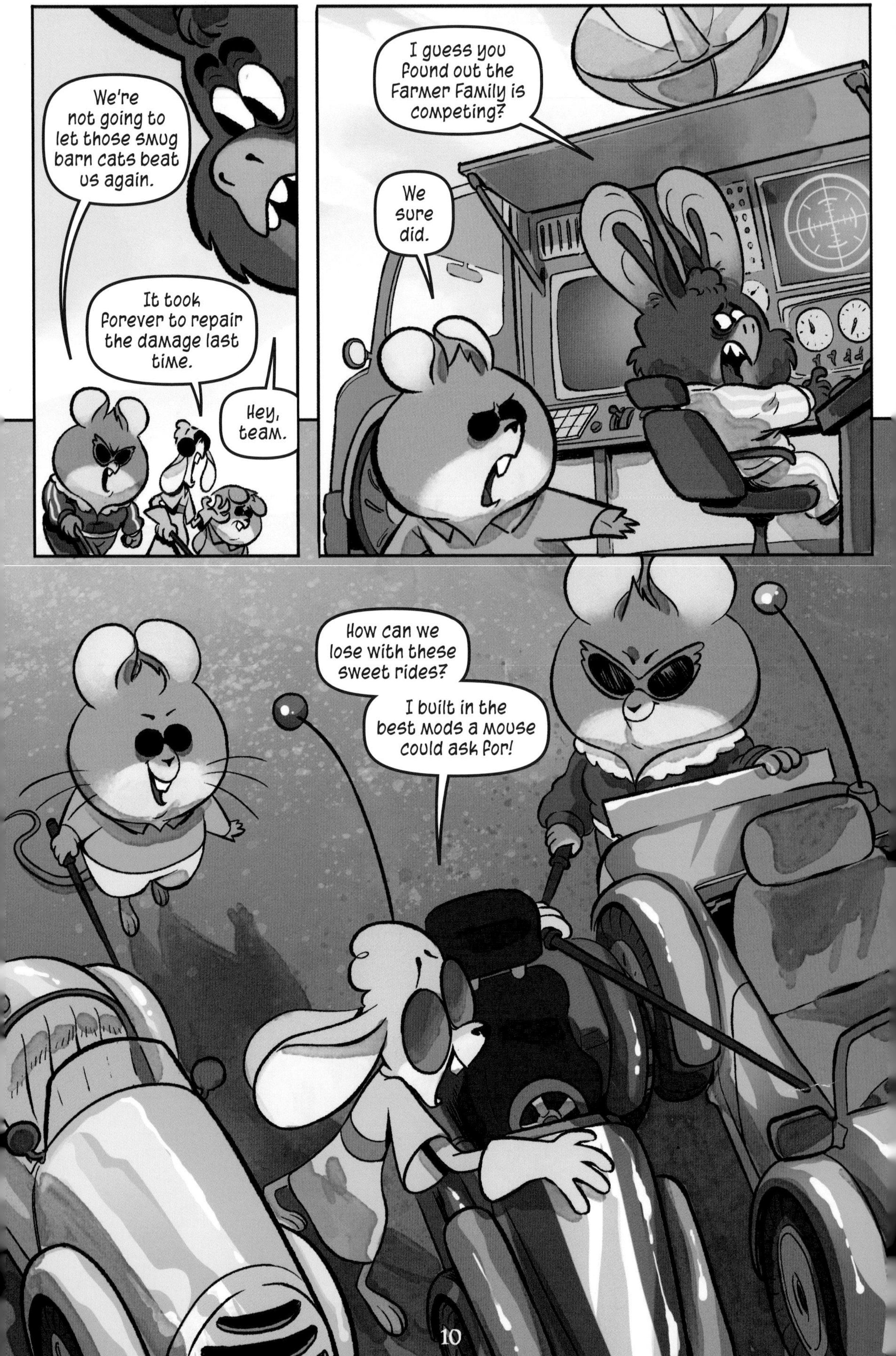
We're not going to let those smug barn cats beat us again.
It took forever to repair the damage last time.
Hey, team.
I guess you found out the Farmer Family is competing?
We sure did.
How can we lose with these sweet rides?
I built in the best mods a mouse could ask for!

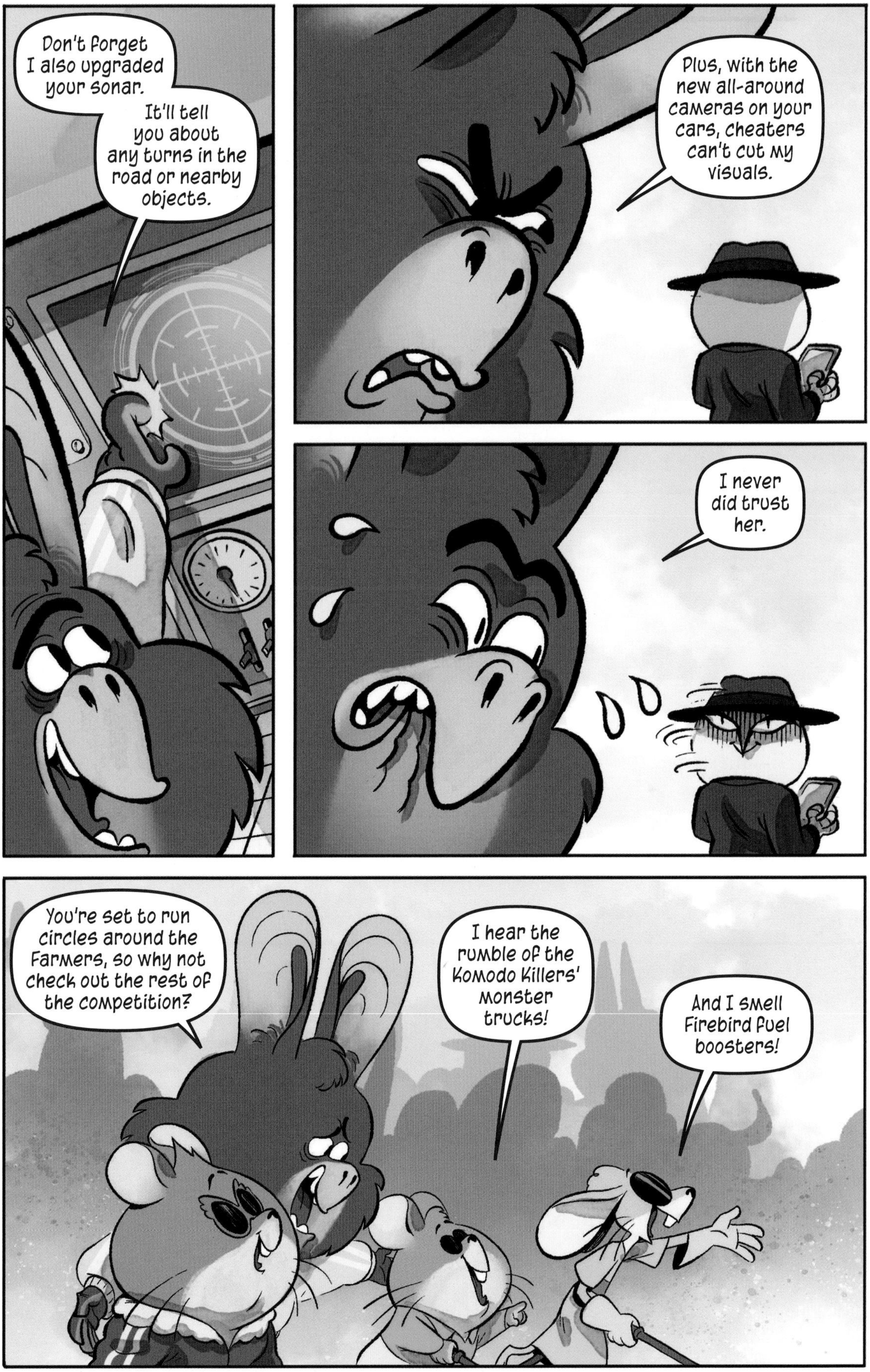
Don't forget I also upgraded your sonar.
It'll tell you about any turns in the road or nearby objects.
Plus, with the new all-around cameras on your cars, cheaters can't cut my visuals.
I never did trust her.
You're set to run circles around the Farmers, so why not check out the rest of the competition?
I hear the rumble of the Komodo Killers' monster trucks!
And I smell Firebird fuel boosters!

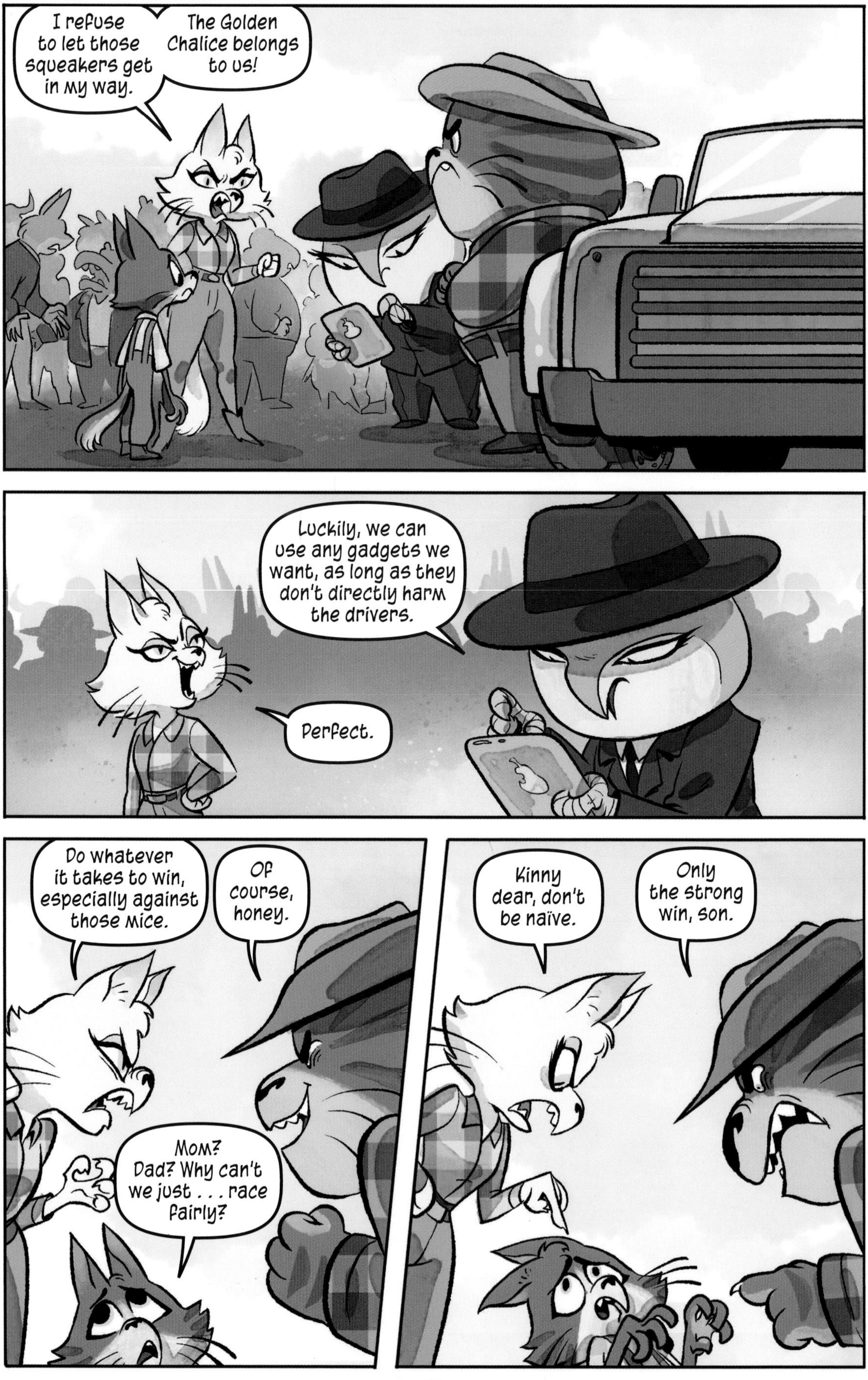
I refuse to let those squeakers get in my way.
The Golden Chalice belongs to us!
Luckily, we can use any gadgets we want, as long as they don't directly harm the drivers.
Perfect.
Do whatever it takes to win, especially against those mice.
Of course, honey.
Mom? Dad? Why can't we just . . . race fairly?
Kinny dear, don't be naïve.
Only the strong win, son.

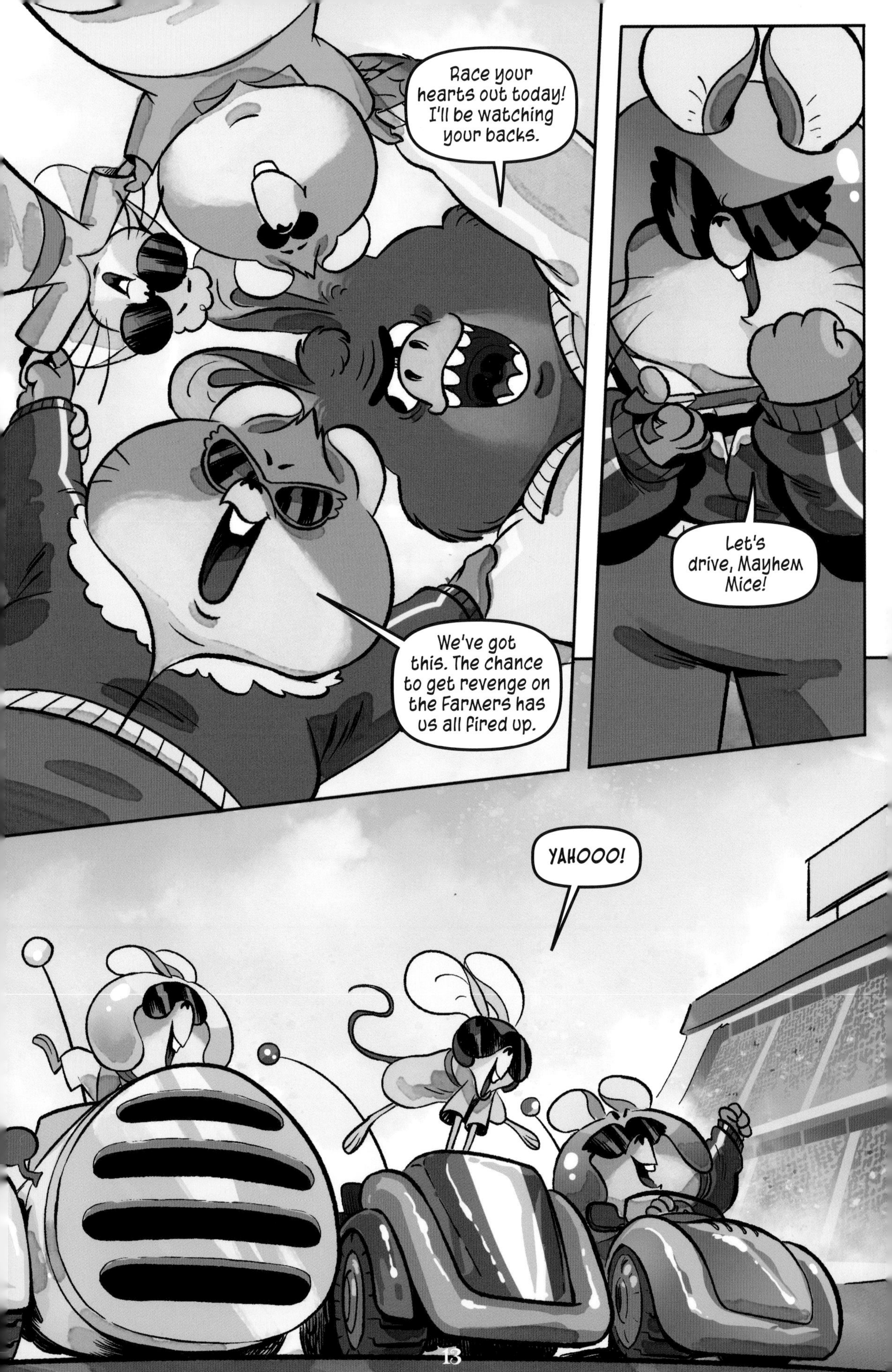
Race your hearts out today! I'll be watching your backs.
We've got this. The chance to get revenge on the Farmers has us all fired up.
Let's drive, Mayhem Mice!
YAHOOO!

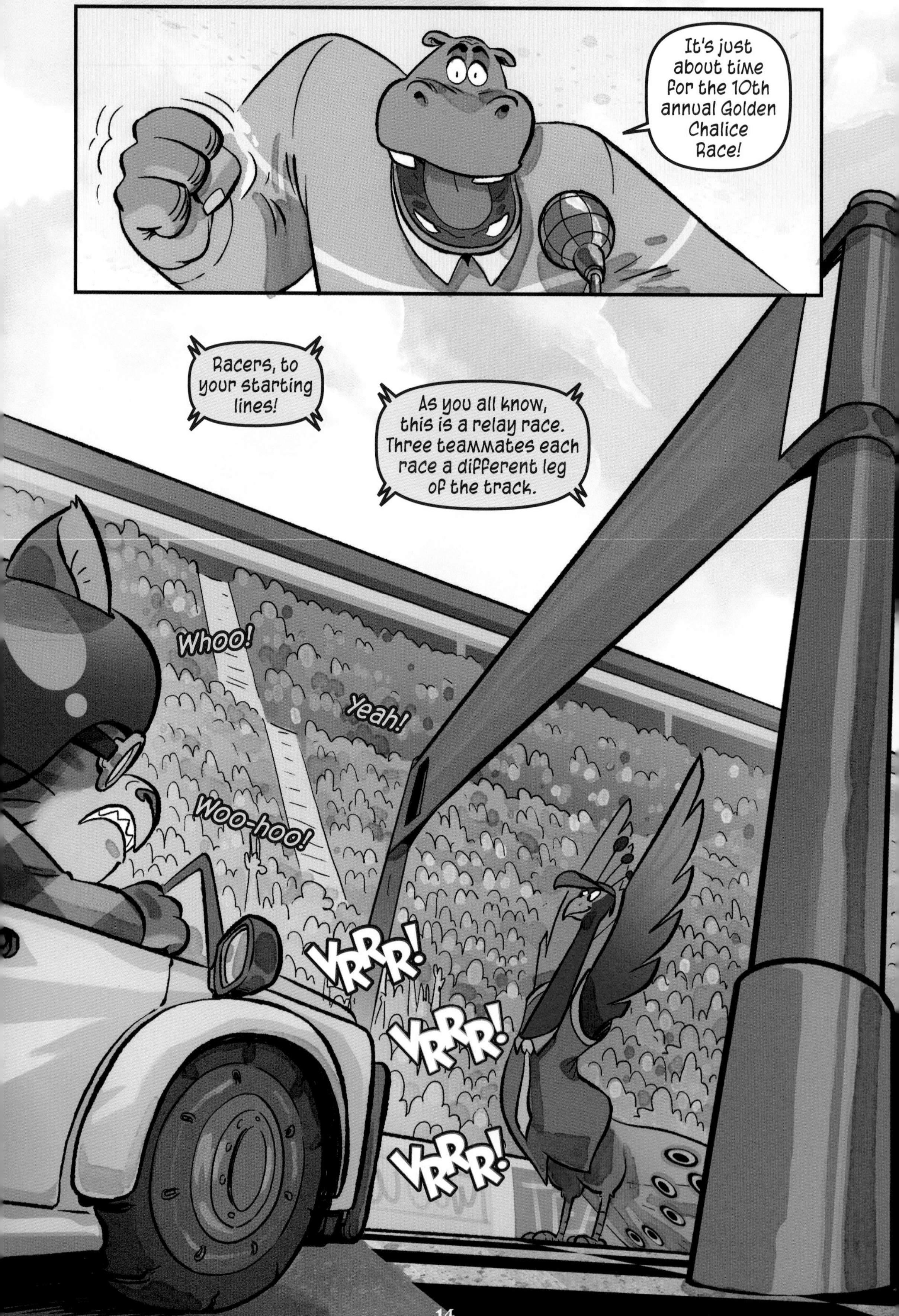
It's just about time for the 10th annual Golden Chalice Race!
Racers, to your starting lines!
As you all know, this is a relay race. Three teammates each race a different leg of the track.
Whoo!
Yeah!
Woo-hoo!
VRRR!
VRRRR!
VRRRR!

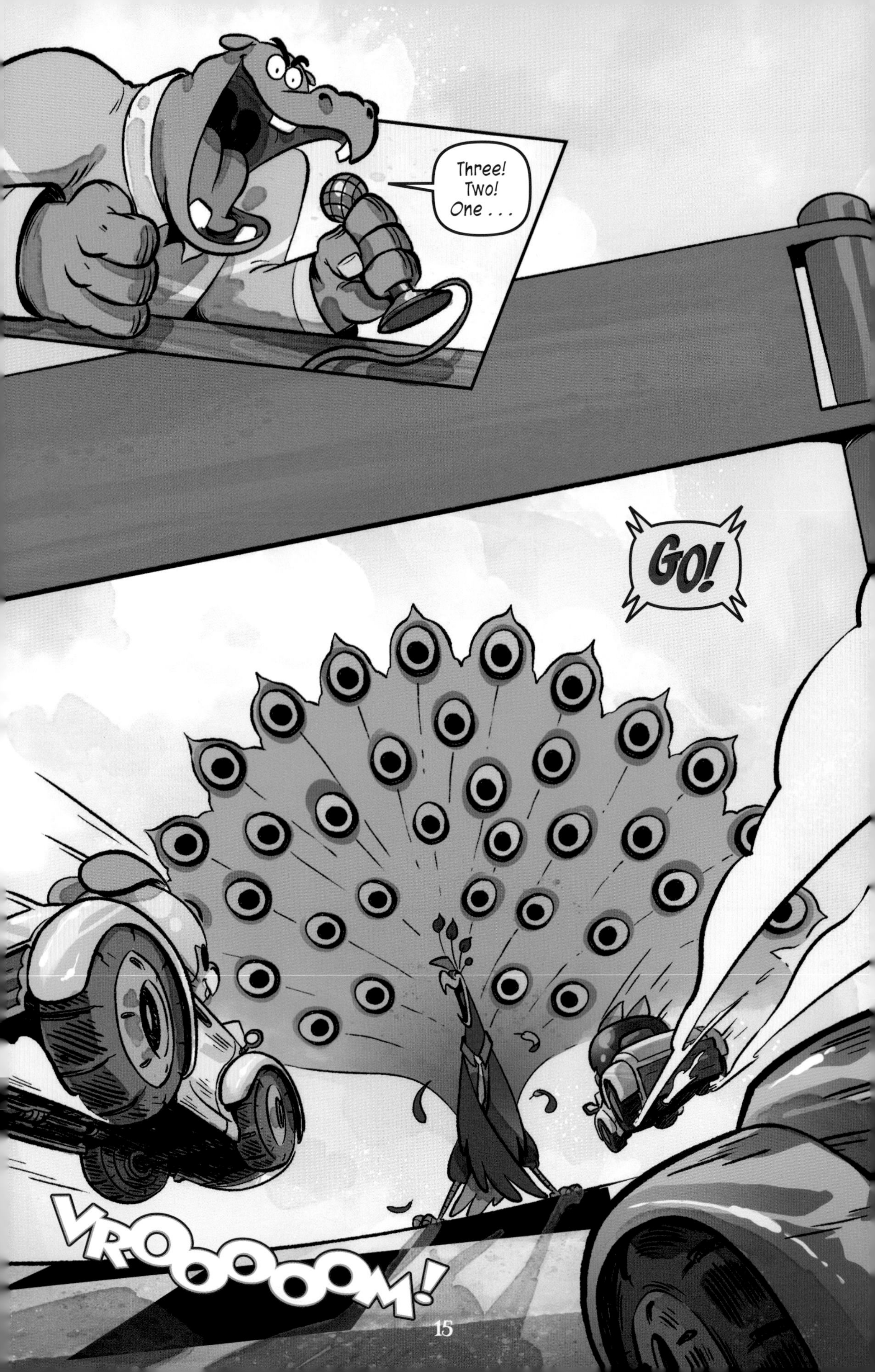
Three! Two! One . . .
GO!
VROOOOOOM!

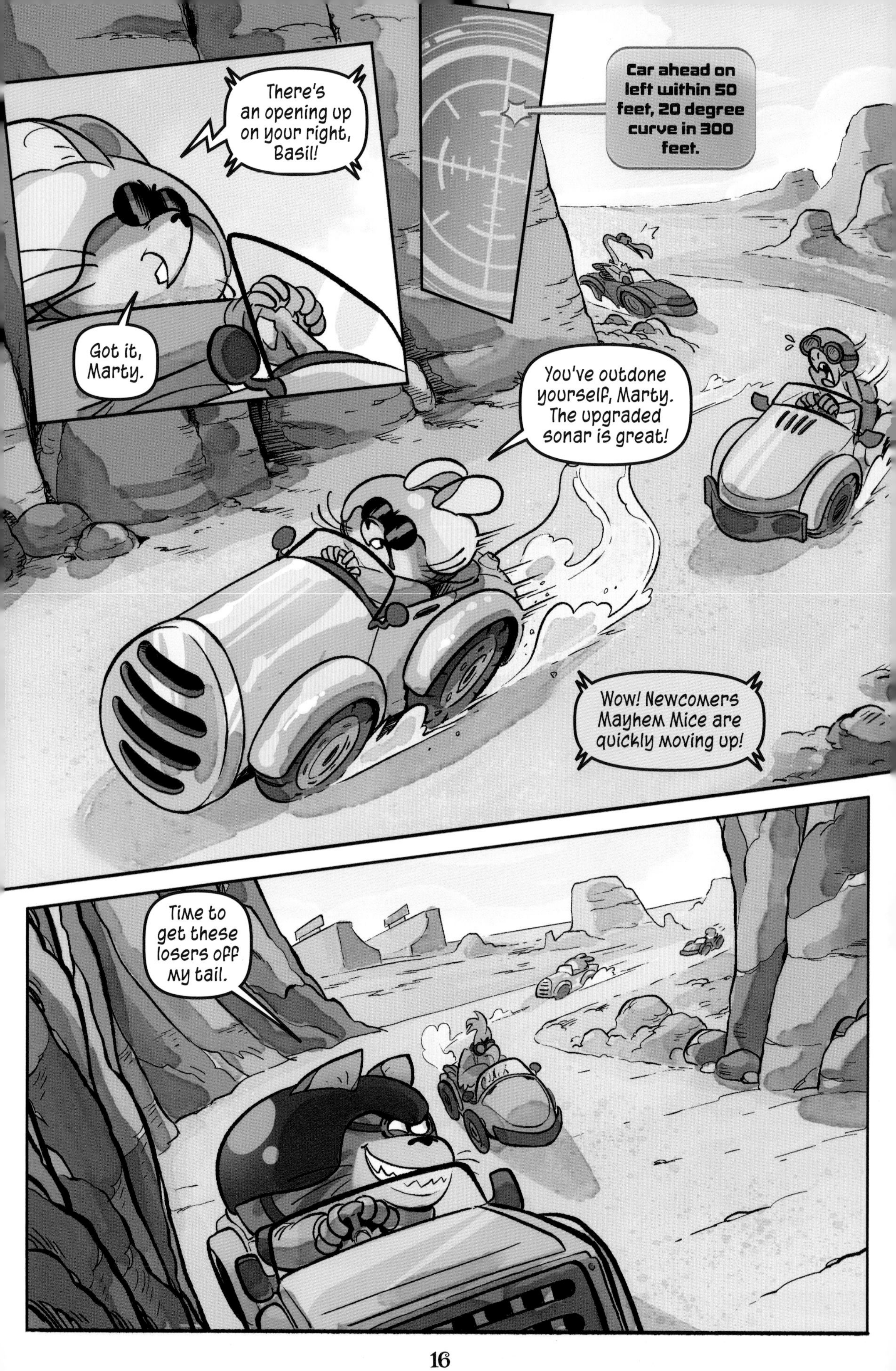
There's an opening up on your right, Basil!
Car ahead on left within 50 feet, 20 degree curve in 300 feet.
Got it, Marty.
You've outdone yourself, Marty. The upgraded sonar is great!
Wow! Newcomers Mayhem Mice are quickly moving up!
Time to get these losers off my tail.

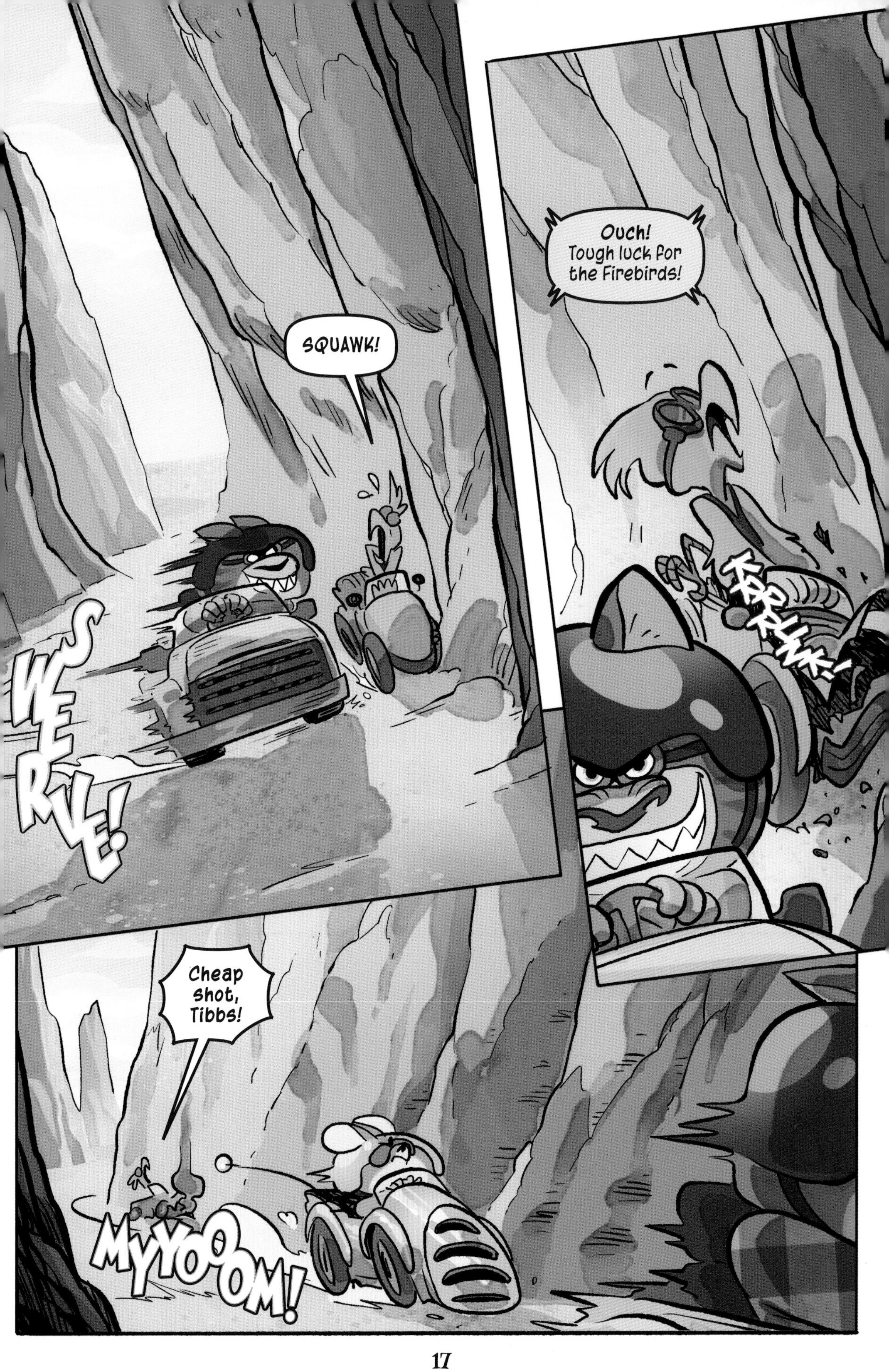
SQUAWK!
SWERVE!
Ouch!
Tough luck for
the Firebirds!
KRRUNK!
Cheap
shot,
Tibbs!
MYYOOOM!

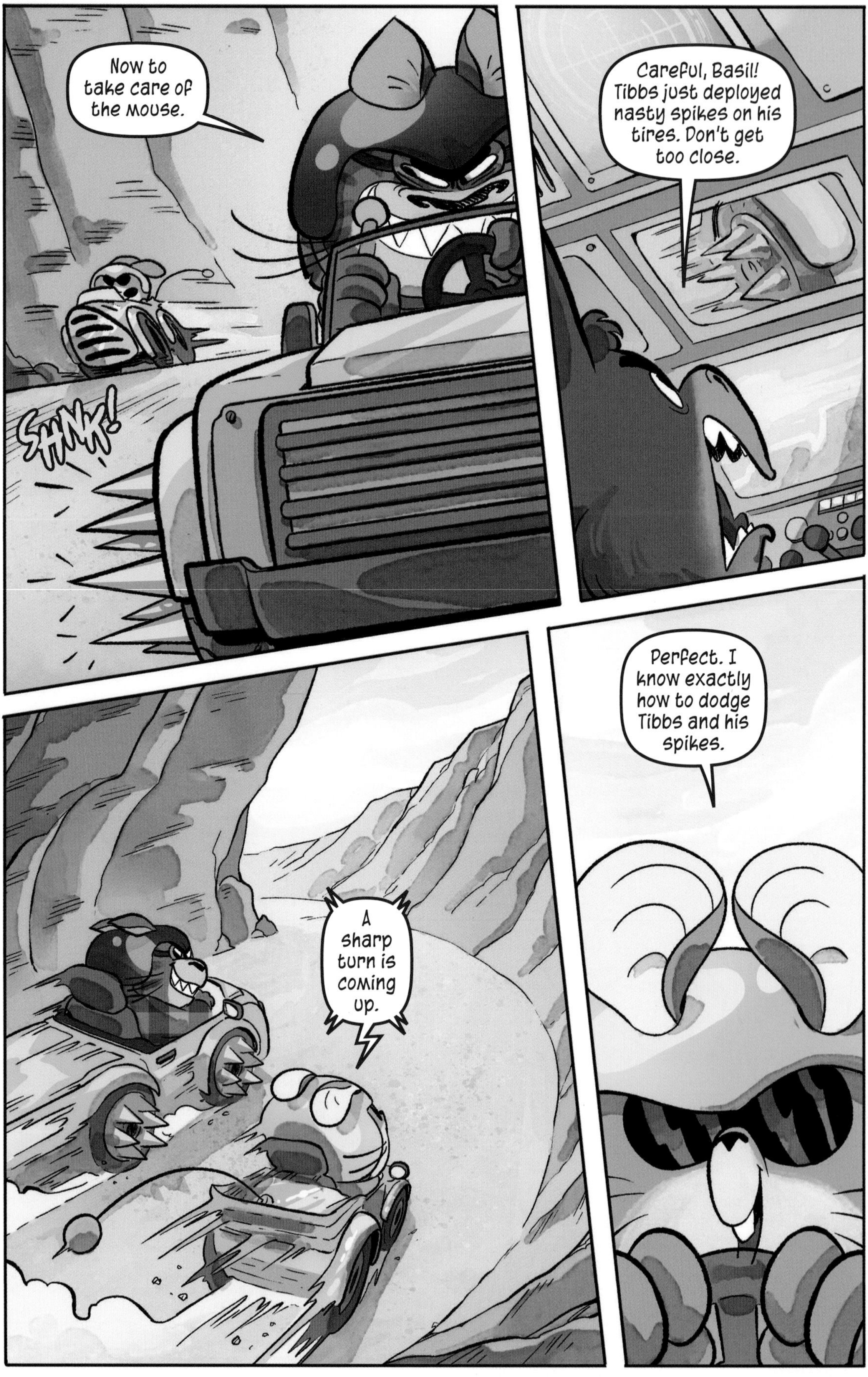
Now to take care of the mouse.
SHNK!
Careful, Basil! Tibbs just deployed nasty spikes on his tires. Don't get too close.
A sharp turn is coming up.
Perfect. I know exactly how to dodge Tibbs and his spikes.

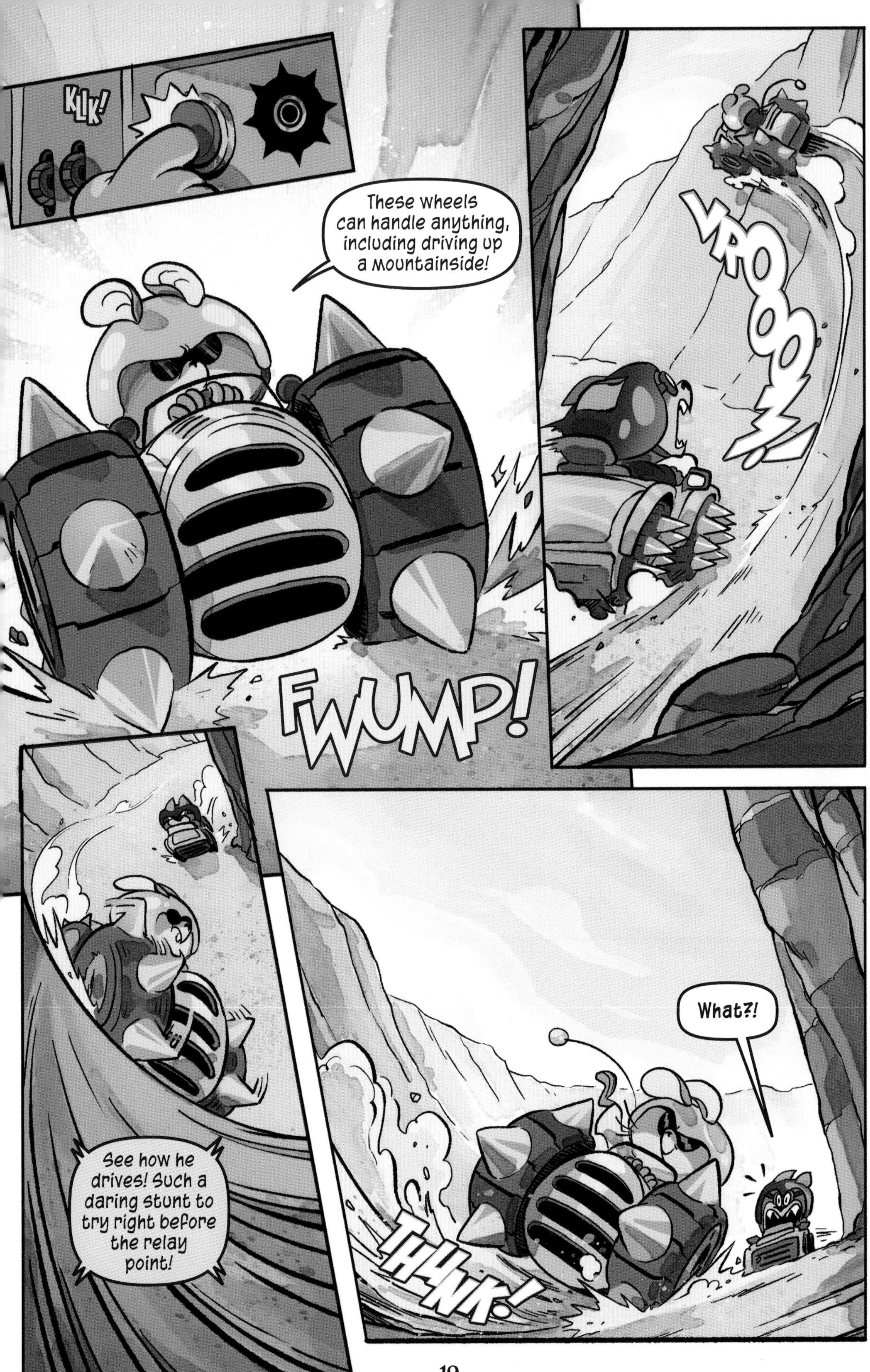
KLIK!
These wheels can handle anything, including driving up a mountainside!
FWUMP!
VROOOOM!
See how he drives! Such a daring stunt to try right before the relay point!
What?!
THUNK!

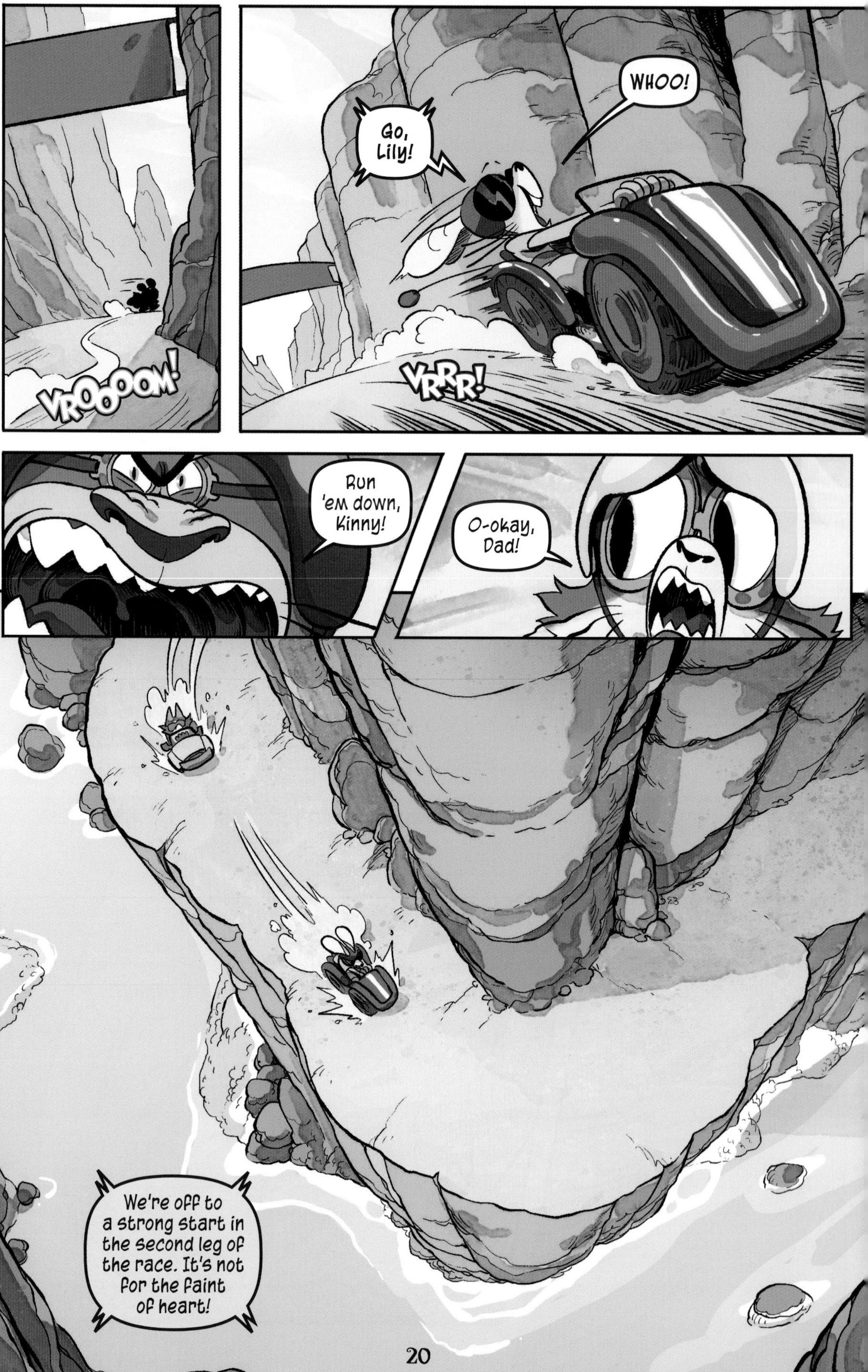
VROOOOM!
Go, Lily!
WHOO!
VRRR!
Run 'em down, Kinny!
O-okay, Dad!
We're off to a strong start in the second leg of the race. It's not for the faint of heart!

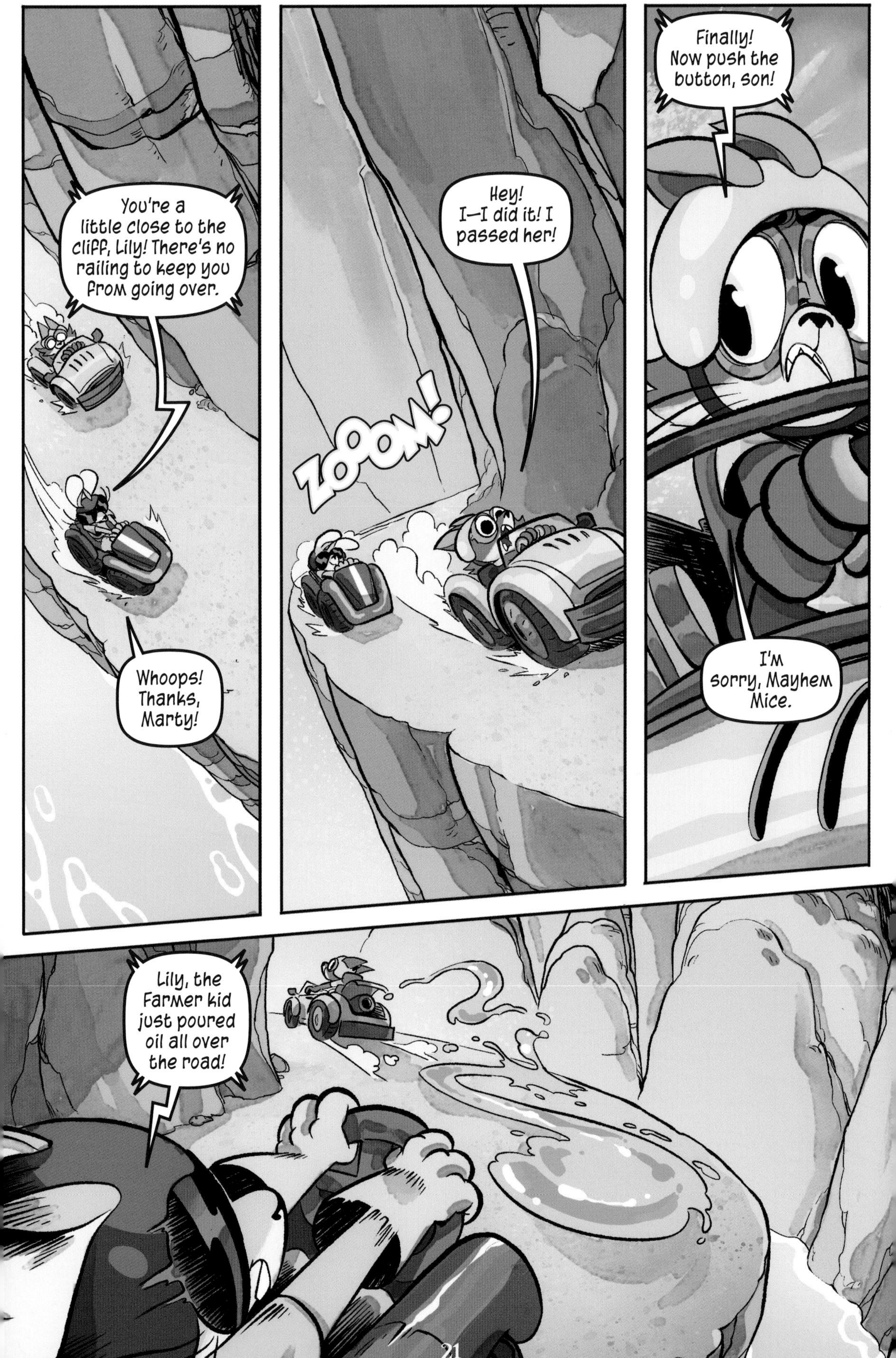
You're a little close to the cliff, Lily! There's no railing to keep you from going over.
Whoops! Thanks, Marty!
ZOOOM!
Hey! I—I did it! I passed her!
Finally! Now push the button, son!
I'm sorry, Mayhem Mice.
Lily, the Farmer kid just poured oil all over the road!

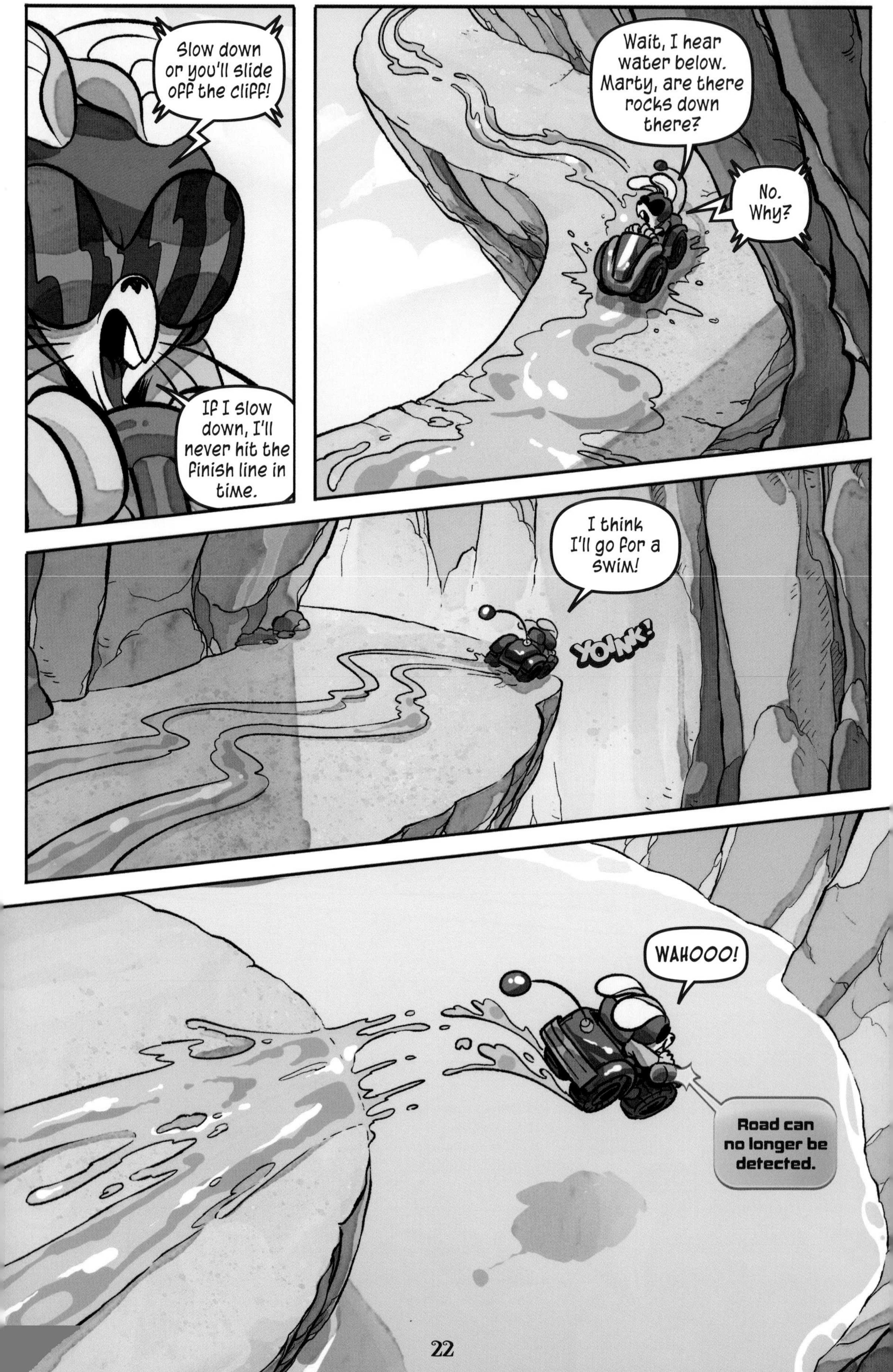
Slow down or you'll slide off the cliff!
If I slow down, I'll never hit the finish line in time.
Wait, I hear water below. Marty, are there rocks down there?
No. Why?
I think I'll go for a swim!
YOINK!
WAHOOO!
Road can no longer be detected.

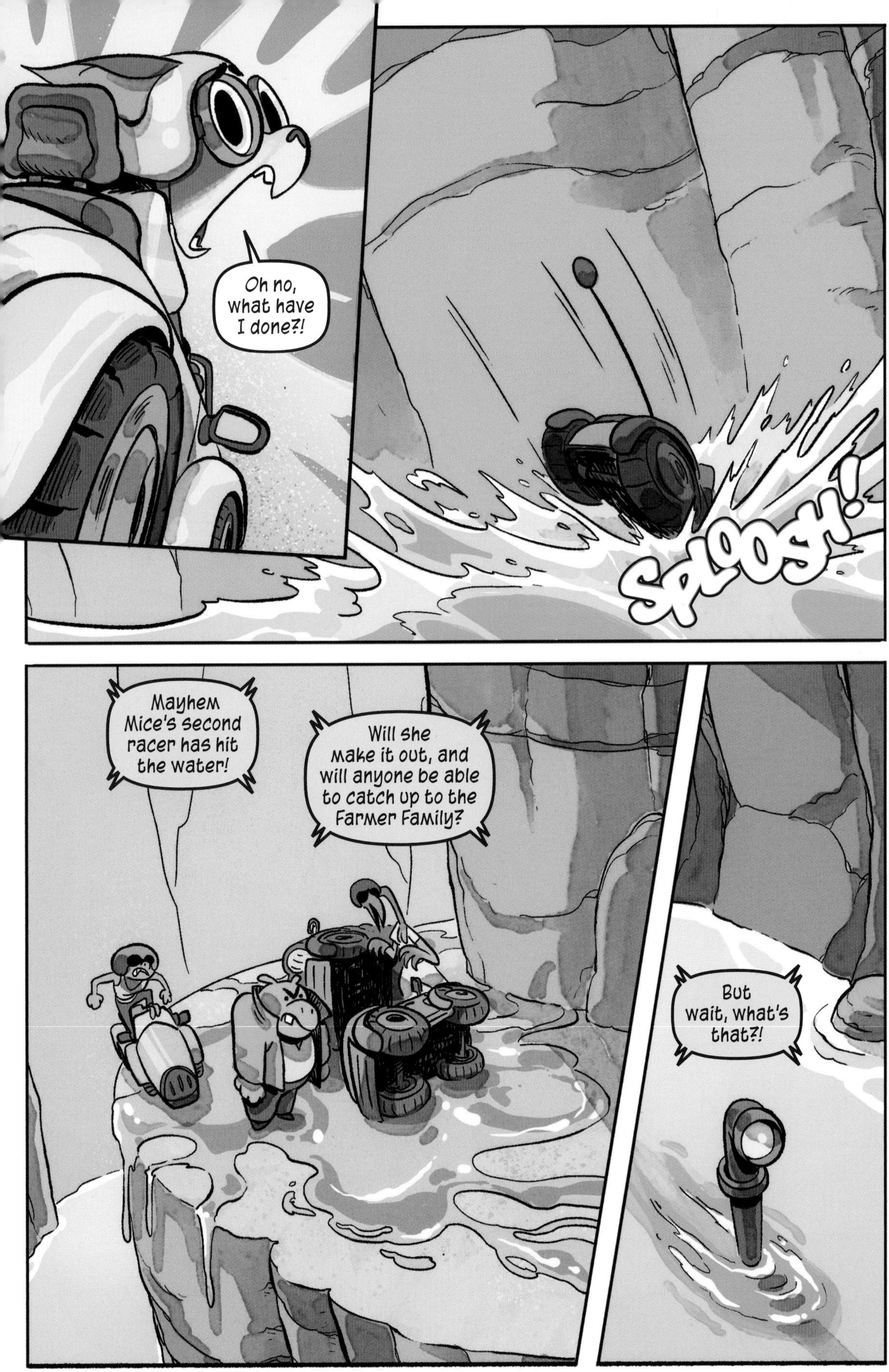
Oh no, what have I done?!
SPLOOSH!
Mayhem Mice's second racer has hit the water!
Will she make it out, and will anyone be able to catch up to the Farmer Family?
But wait, what's that?!

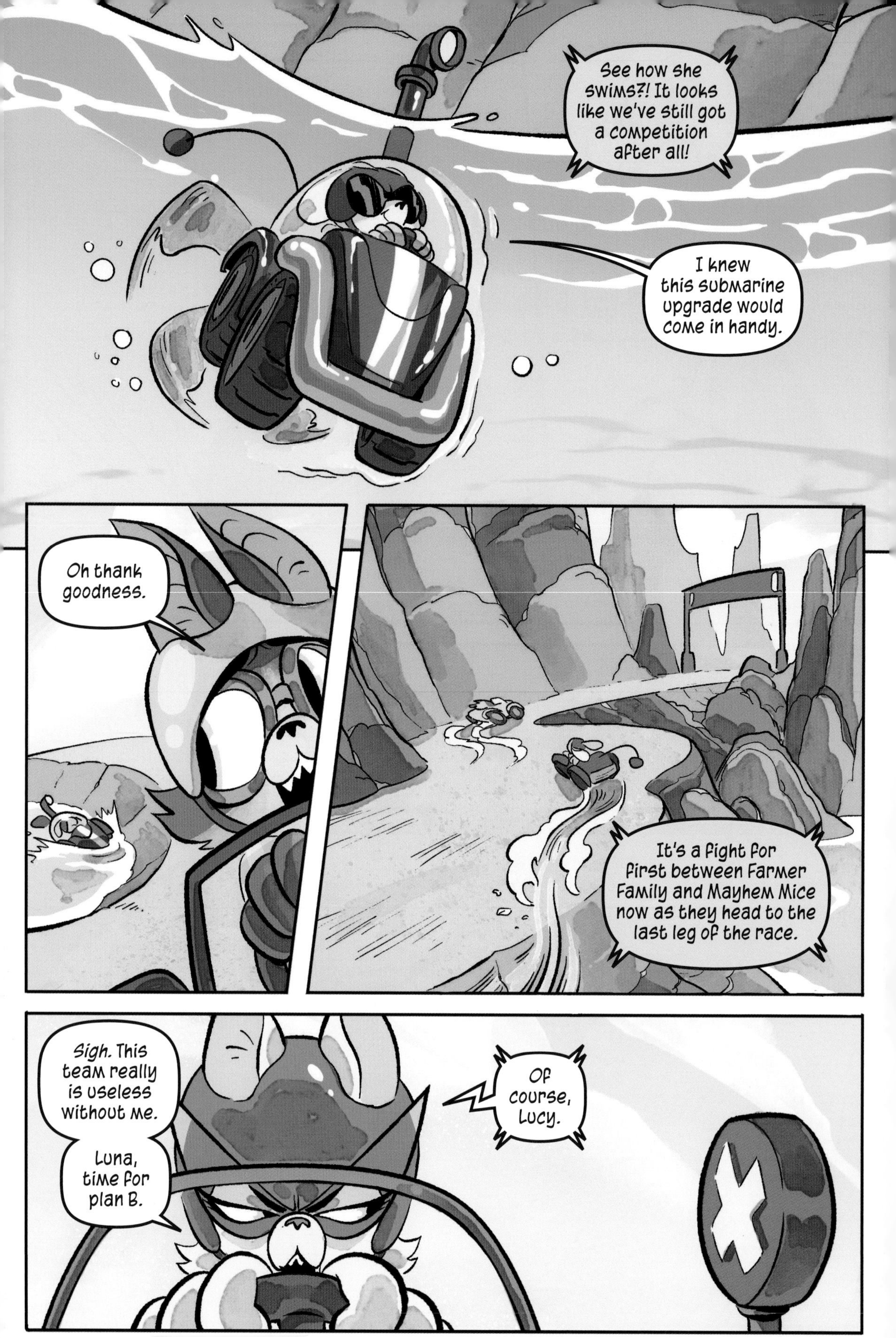
See how she swims?! It looks like we've still got a competition after all!
I knew this submarine upgrade would come in handy.
Oh thank goodness.
It's a fight for first between Farmer Family and Mayhem Mice now as they head to the last leg of the race.
Sigh. This team really is useless without me.
Luna, time for plan B.
Of course, Lucy.

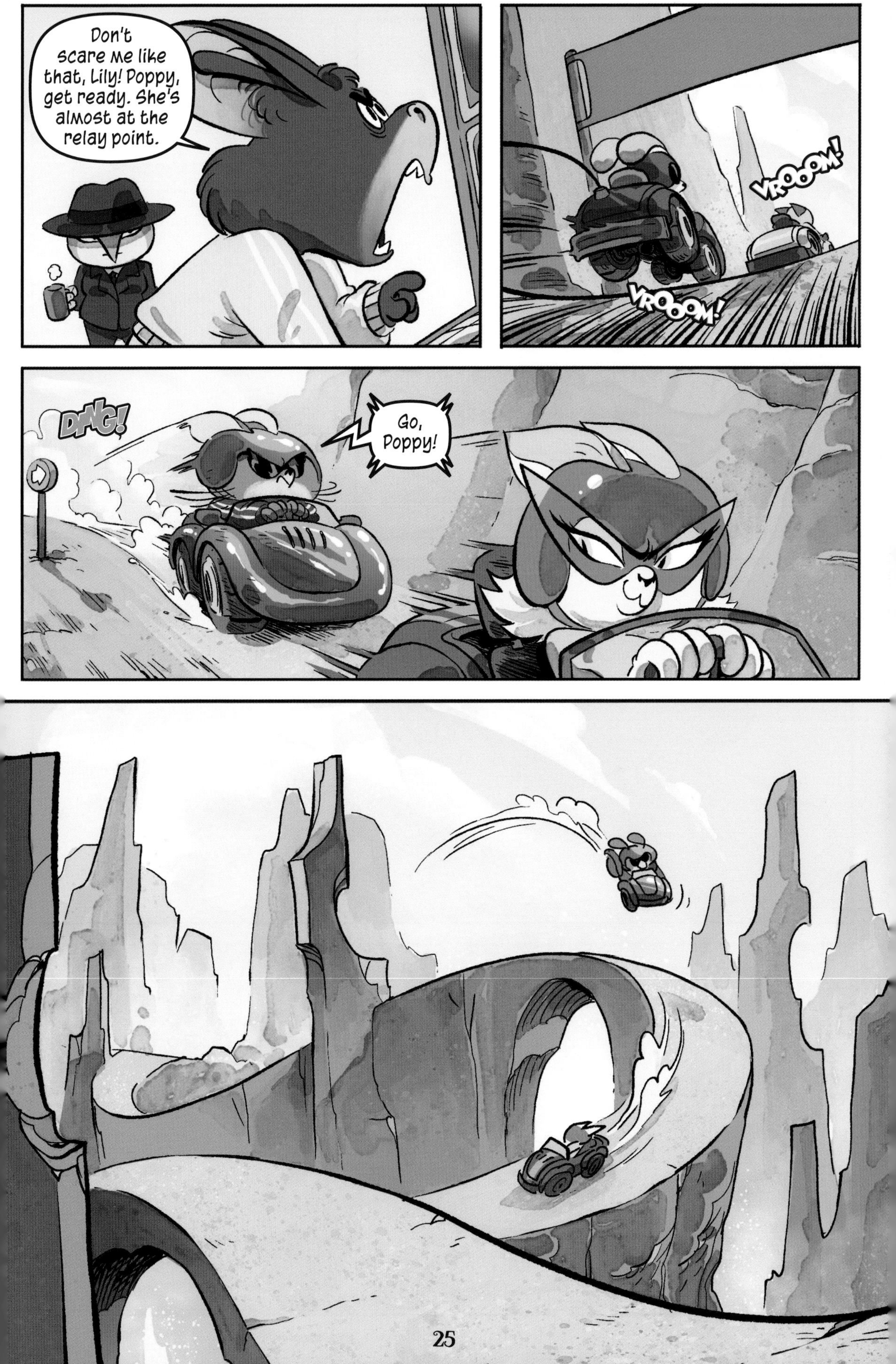
Don't scare me like that, Lily! Poppy, get ready. She's almost at the relay point.
VROOOM!
VROOOM!
DING!
Go, Poppy!

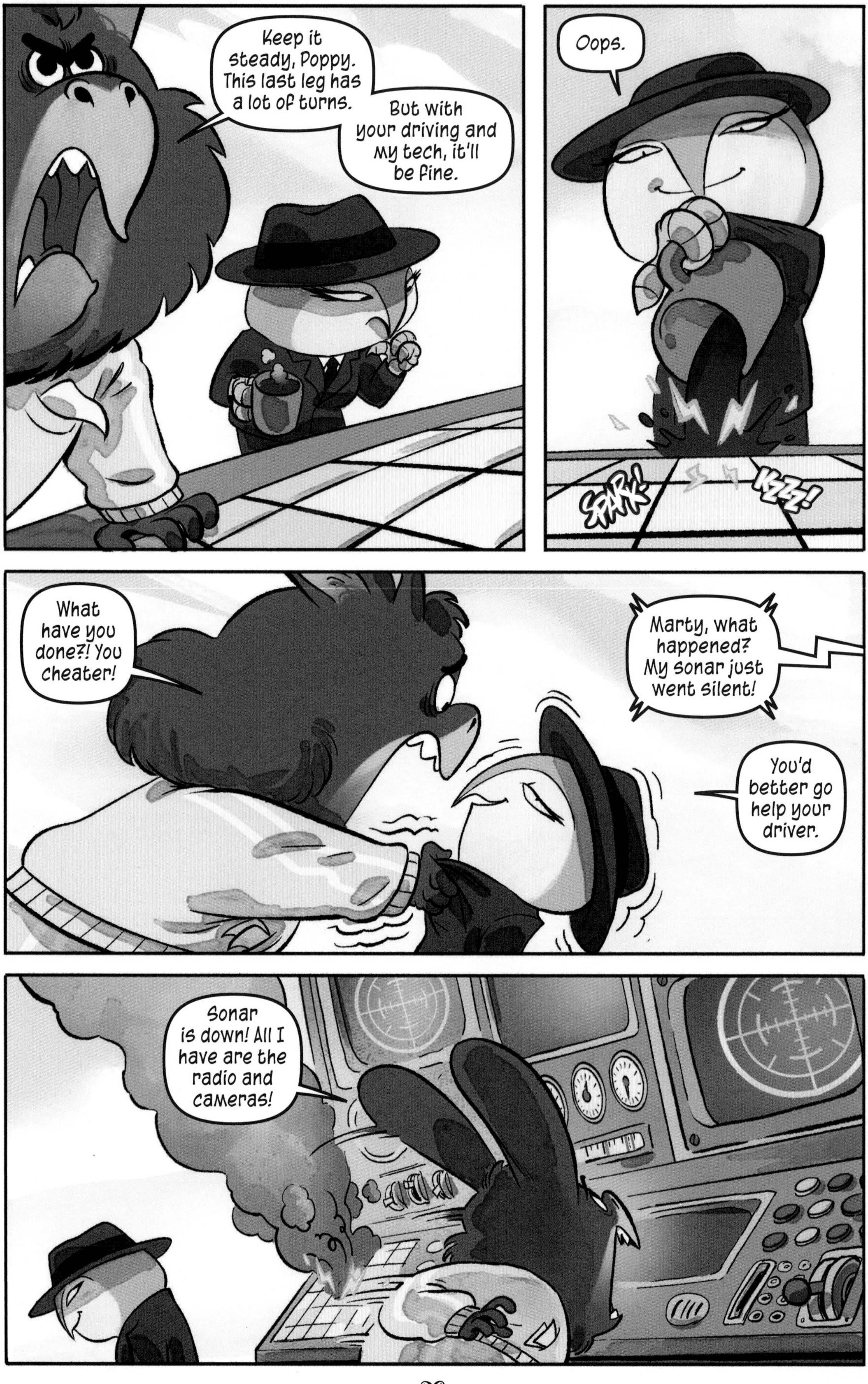

Keep it steady, Poppy. This last leg has a lot of turns.
But with your driving and my tech, it'll be fine.
Oops.
SPARK!
KZZZ!
What have you done?! You cheater!
Marty, what happened? My sonar just went silent!
You'd better go help your driver.
Sonar is down! All I have are the radio and cameras!

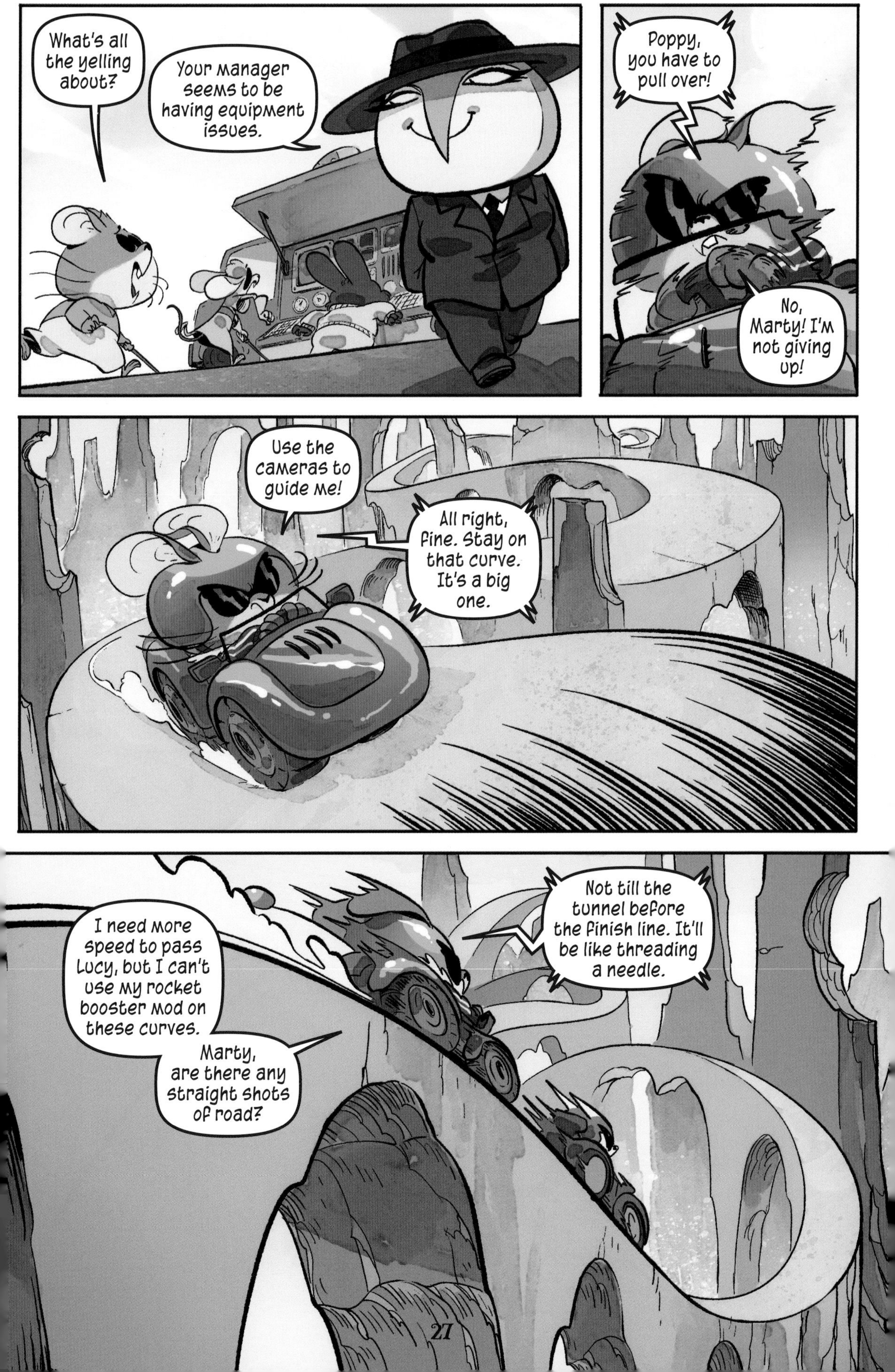
What's all the yelling about?
Your manager seems to be having equipment issues.
Poppy, you have to pull over!
No, Marty! I'm not giving up!
Use the cameras to guide me!
All right, fine. Stay on that curve. It's a big one.
I need more speed to pass Lucy, but I can't use my rocket booster mod on these curves.
Marty, are there any straight shots of road?
Not till the tunnel before the finish line. It'll be like threading a needle.

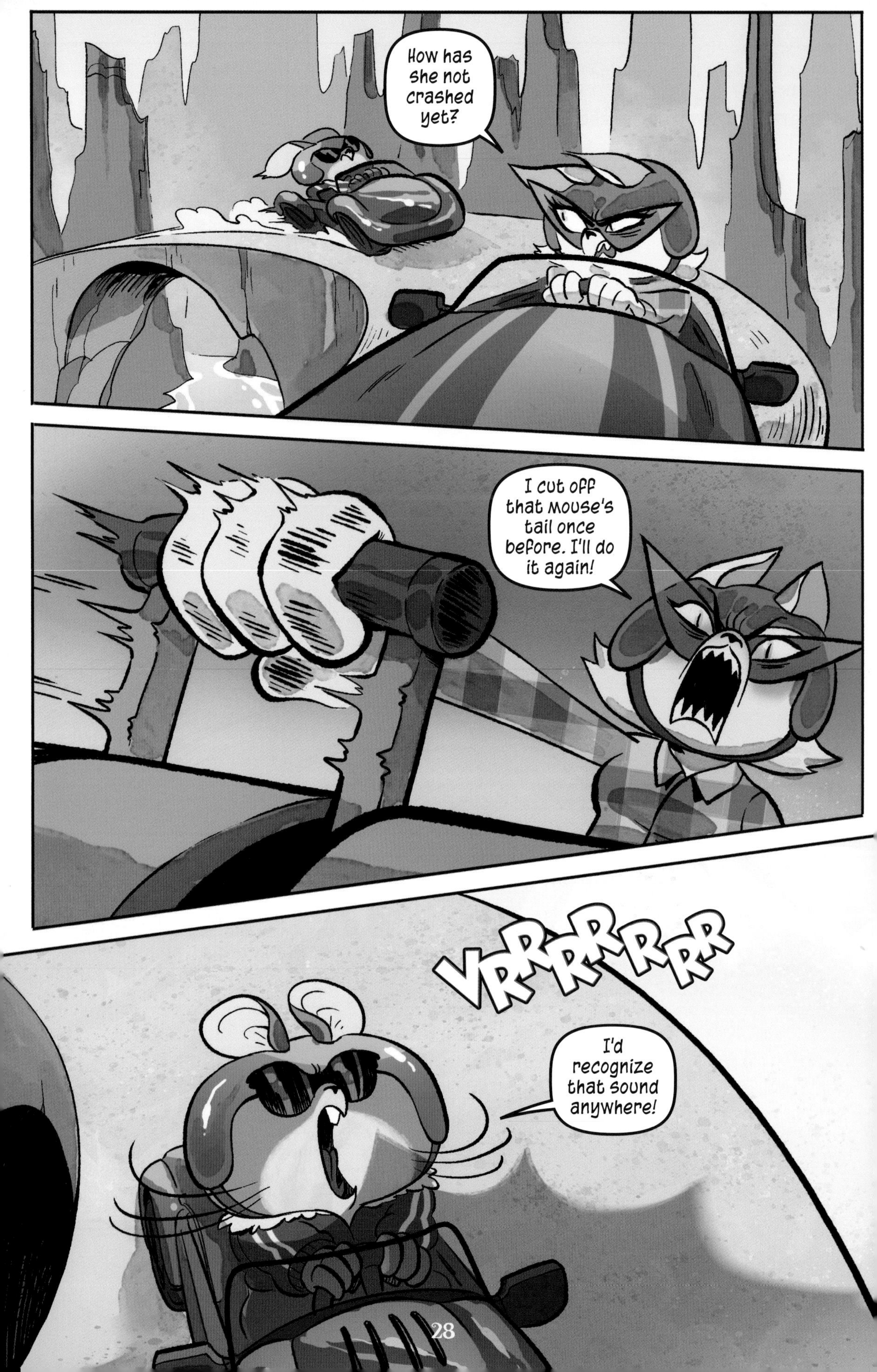

How has she not crashed yet?
I cut off that mouse's tail once before. I'll do it again!
VRRRRRRR
I'd recognize that sound anywhere!

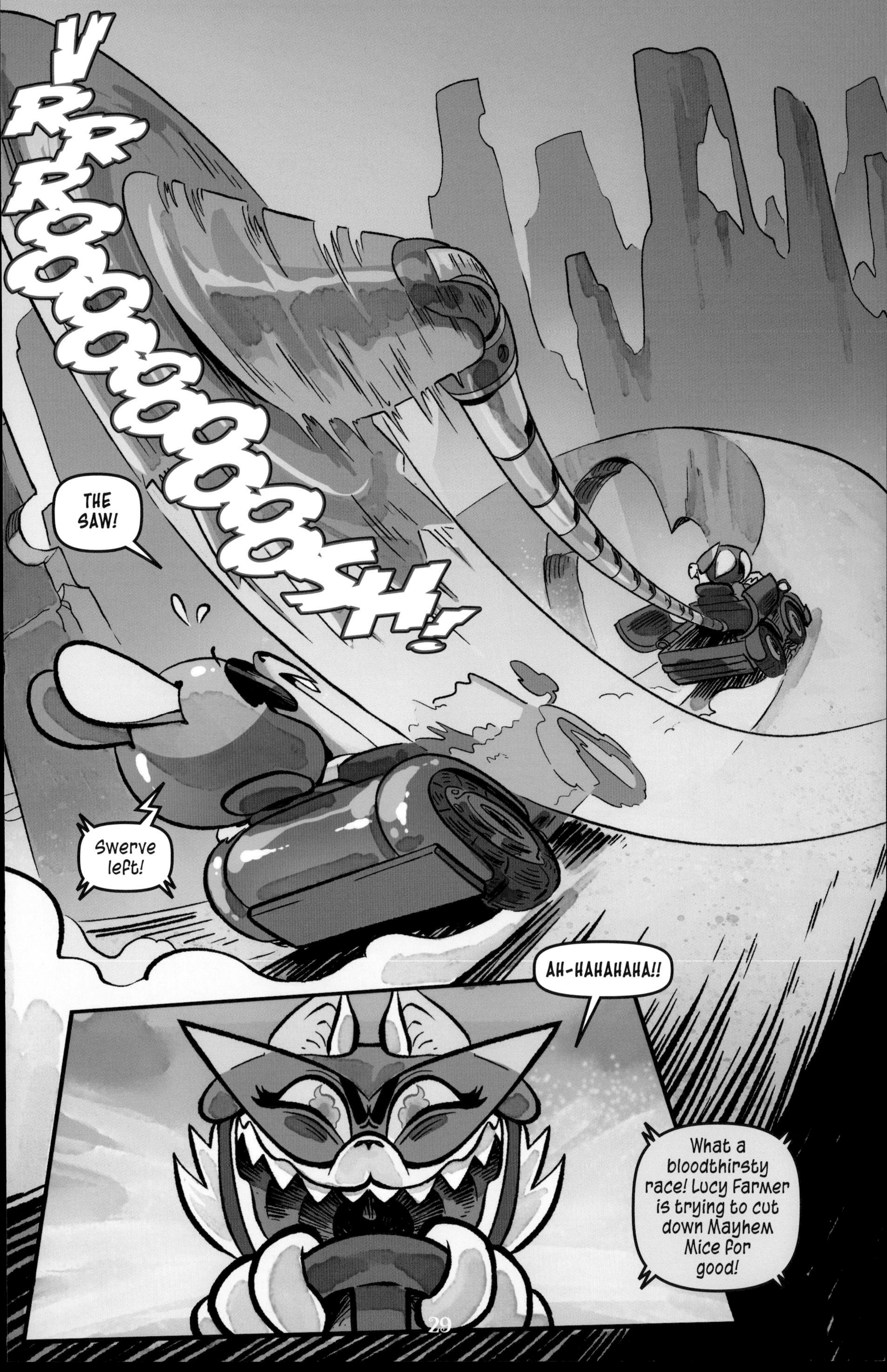
VRRROOOOOOOOOOOOOOOOH!!
THE SAW!
Swerve left!
AH-HAHAHAHA!!
What a bloodthirsty race! Lucy Farmer is trying to cut down Mayhem Mice for good!

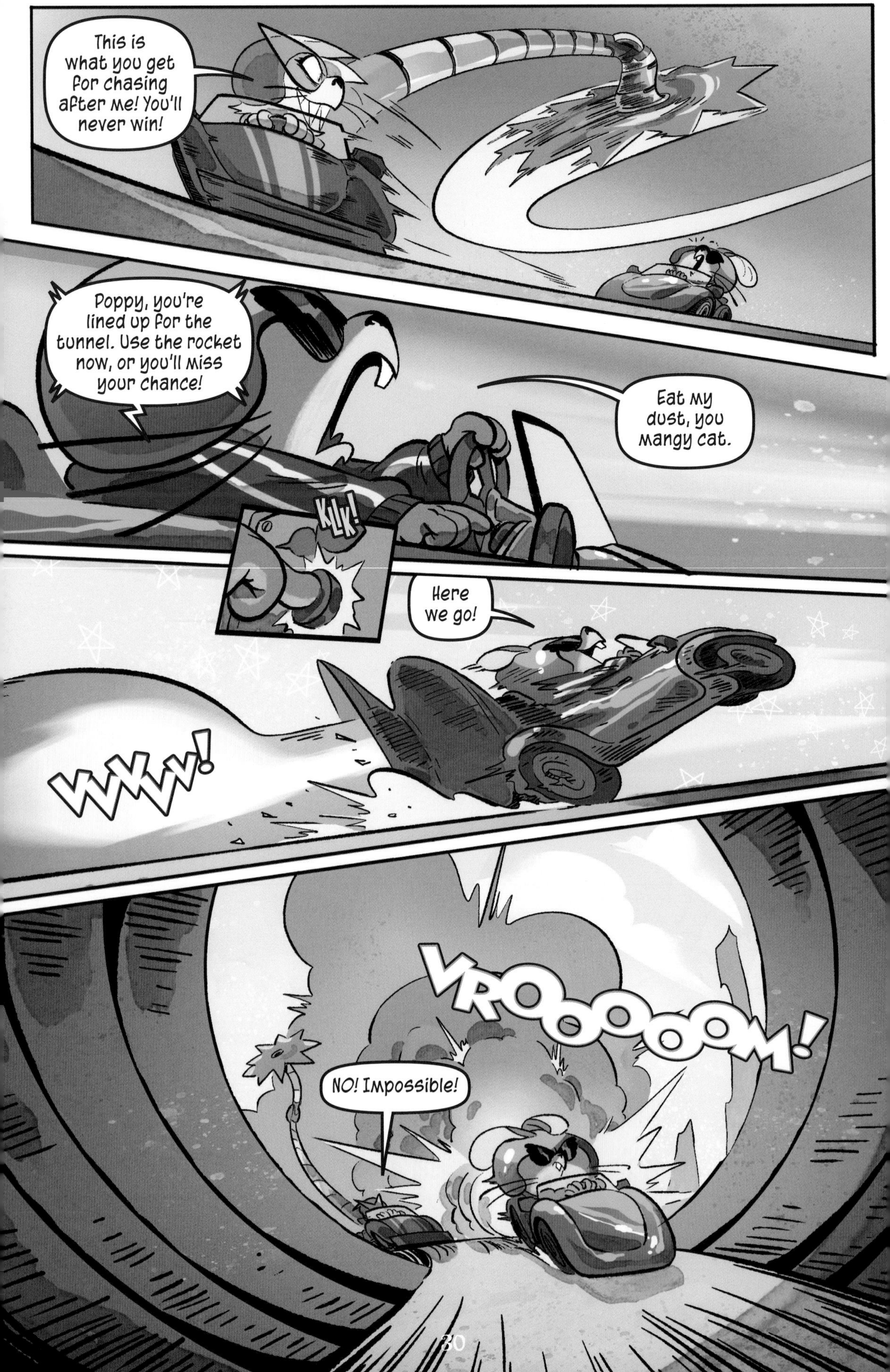
This is what you get for chasing after me! You'll never win!
Poppy, you're lined up for the tunnel. Use the rocket now, or you'll miss your chance!
Eat my dust, you mangy cat.
KLIK!
Here we go!
WVVV!
VROOOOOOM!
NO! Impossible!

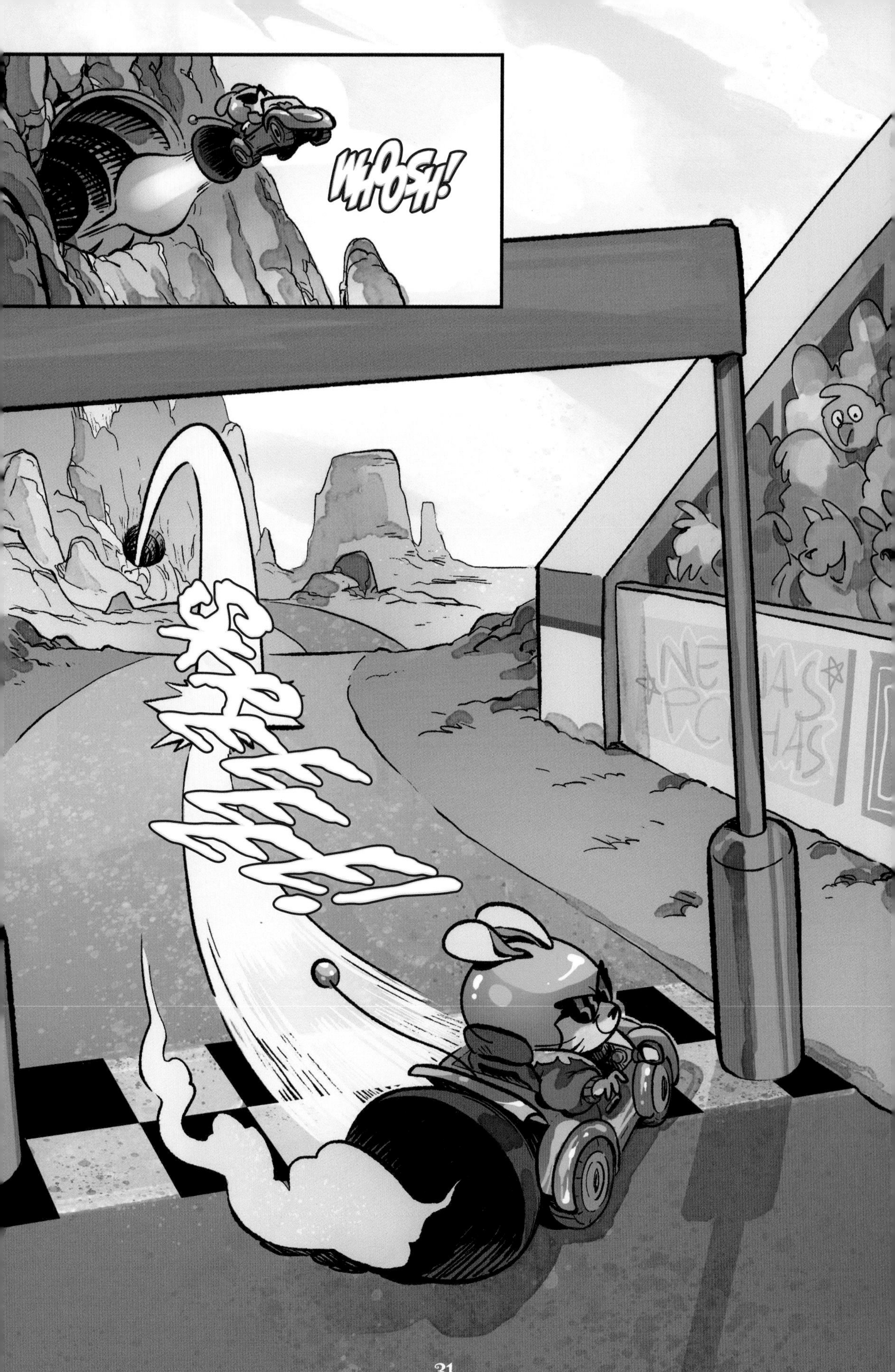
WHOOSH!
SKREEEE!

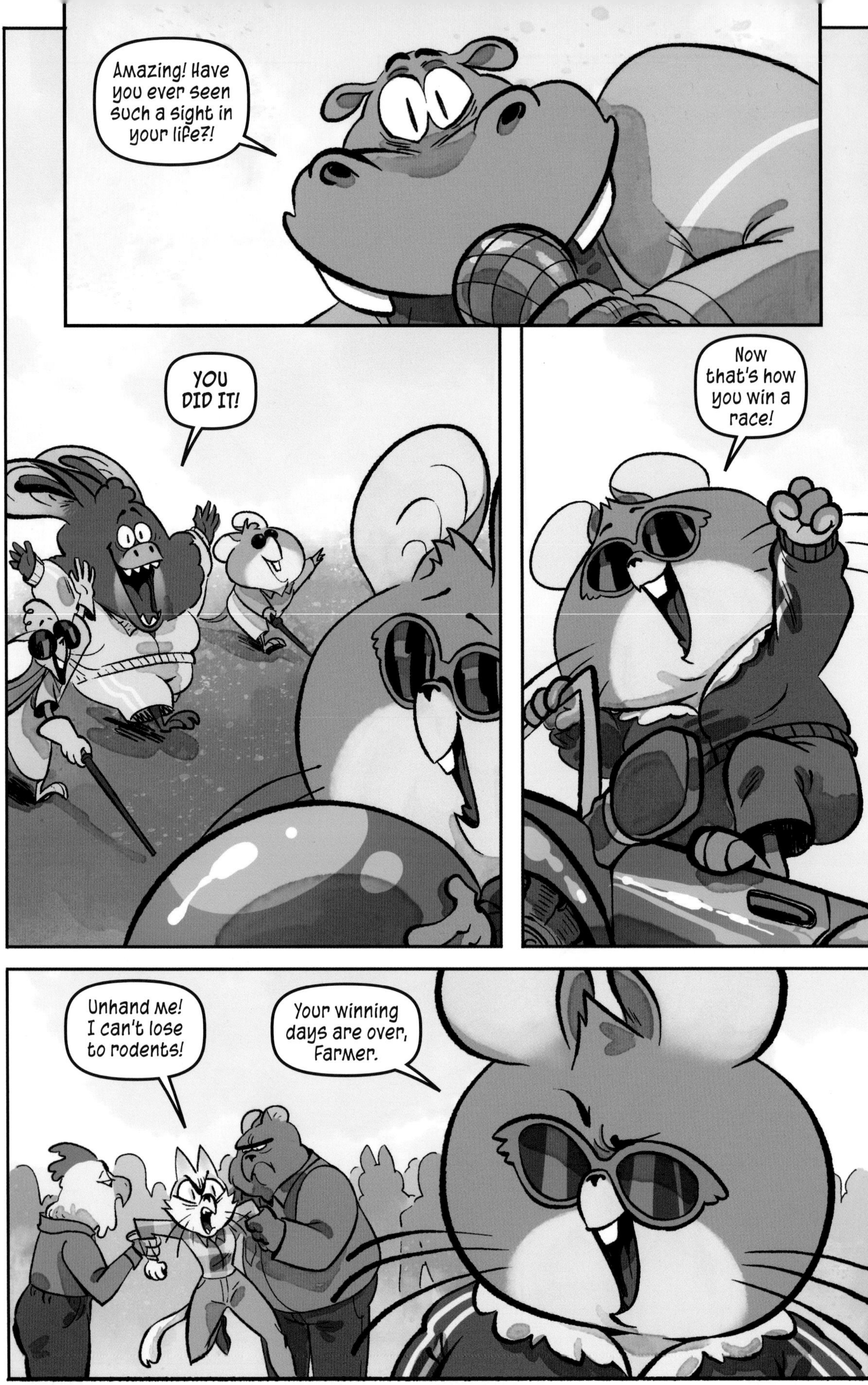
Amazing! Have you ever seen such a sight in your life?!
YOU DID IT!
Now that's how you win a race!
Unhand me! I can't lose to rodents!
Your winning days are over, Farmer.

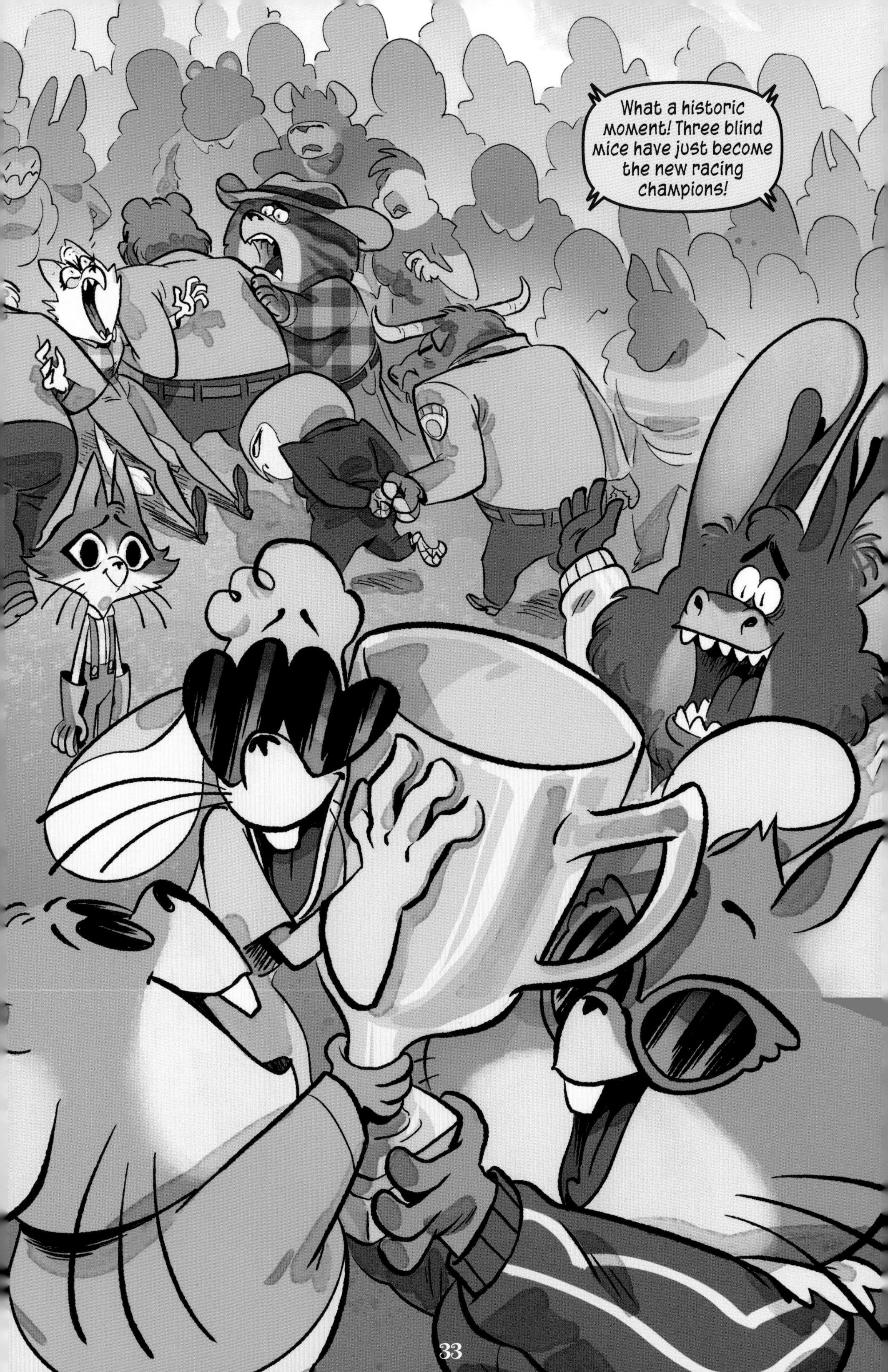
What a historic moment! Three blind mice have just become the new racing champions!

ALL ABOUT THE ORIGINAL TALE!

The original "Three Blind Mice" is a pretty simple tale. In fact, it's not even a full story, but rather a short nursery rhyme often sung to a tune. One of the first known versions was published in the 1600s. Although, the rhyme might have been around before then and just hadn't been written down.

There is also a longer, "complete" story that was published in 1904. It follows three mischievous mice who go out looking for adventure. But when they visit a farmer to ask for food, the farmer's wife sends her cat after them! The three fall into thorny bramble bushes, which blinds them. If that's not bad enough, the farmer's wife then chops off the mice's tails! In the end, the clever rodents find medicine that heals their eyes and regrows their tales, and they settle down to live quiet lives.

But the most well-known version of the rhyme goes like this:

Three blind mice, three blind mice,
See how they run, see how they run,
They all ran after the farmer's wife,
Who cut of their tails with a carving knife,
Did you ever see such a sight in your life,
As three blind mice?

The great thing about something so simple and catchy is that it's easy to remember, which has helped "Three Blind Mice" stick around for so long. Just imagine, you could sing almost the same rhyme as a kid from more than four hundred years ago!

A **FAR OUT** GUIDE TO THE TALE'S RACING TWISTS!

The farmer's wife became Lucy Farmer, a cat. In fact, everyone gets to be animals, because it's just more fun that way.

Instead of cutting off tails with a carving knife, Lucy Farmer cuts off the end of Poppy's racing car with a giant saw.

The mice don't run after the farmer's wife. They chase the Farmer Family team, including Tibbs and Kinny, for the racing title!

In the original rhyme, the mice were normal rodents. Here, they're daredevil racers!

VISUAL QUESTIONS

Sound effects are used throughout the story to help add to the action. Which one is your favorite? Why? Try designing your own!

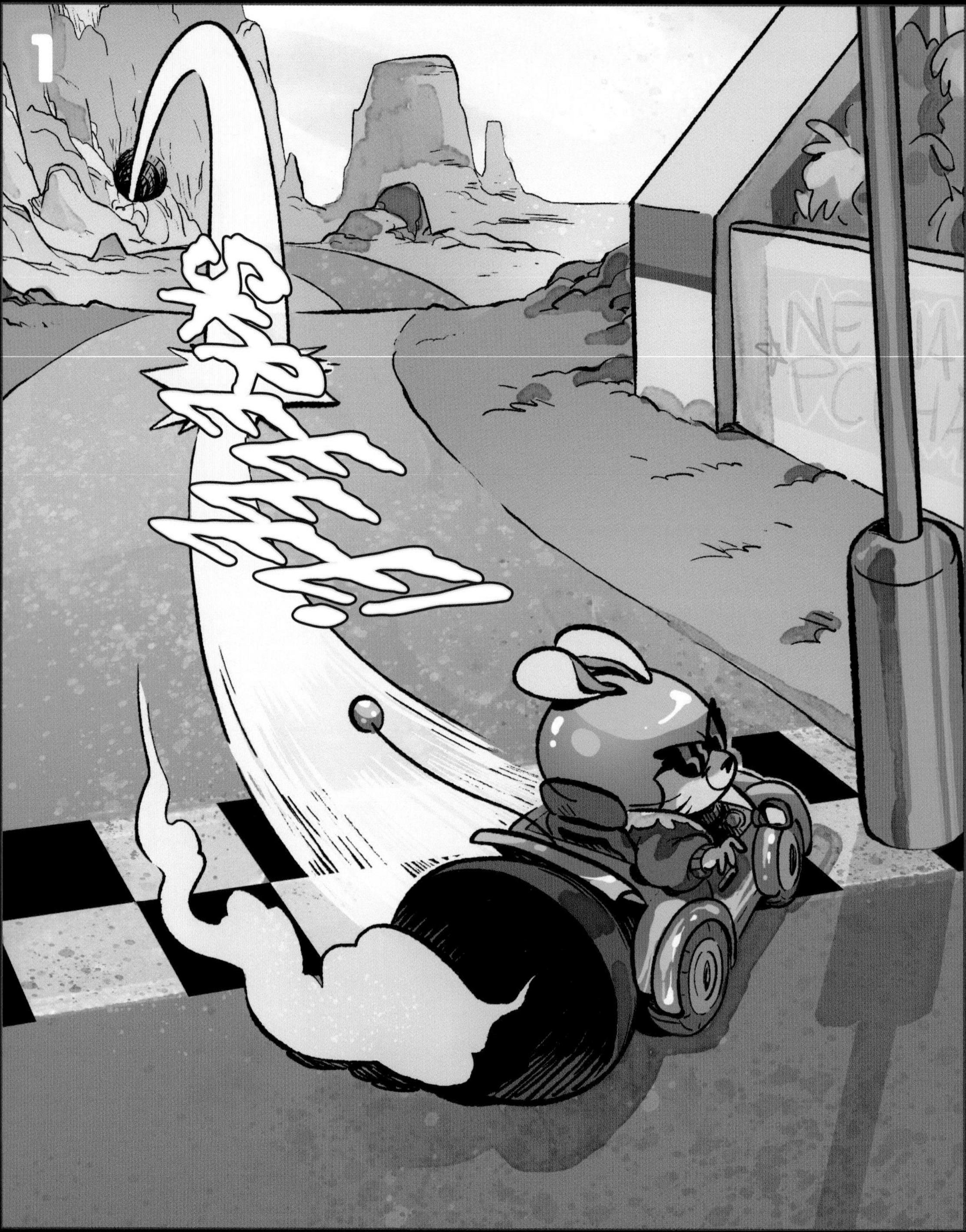
1
SKREEE!

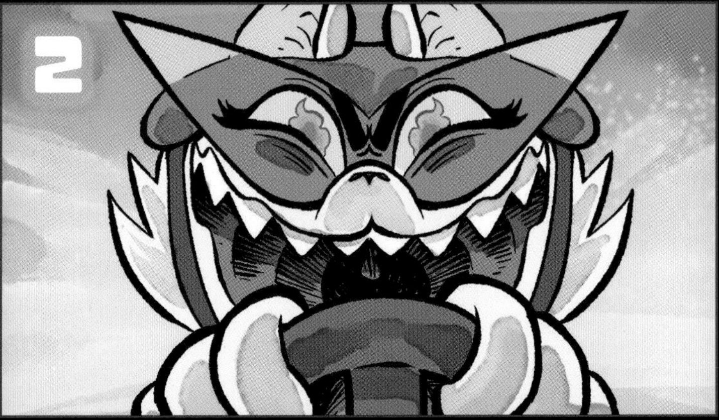
2

Why are there flames in Lucy's eyes? How would you describe her feelings in this moment?

What is Lily doing in this panel from page 22? Describe the scene in your own words. Were you surprised by her choice?

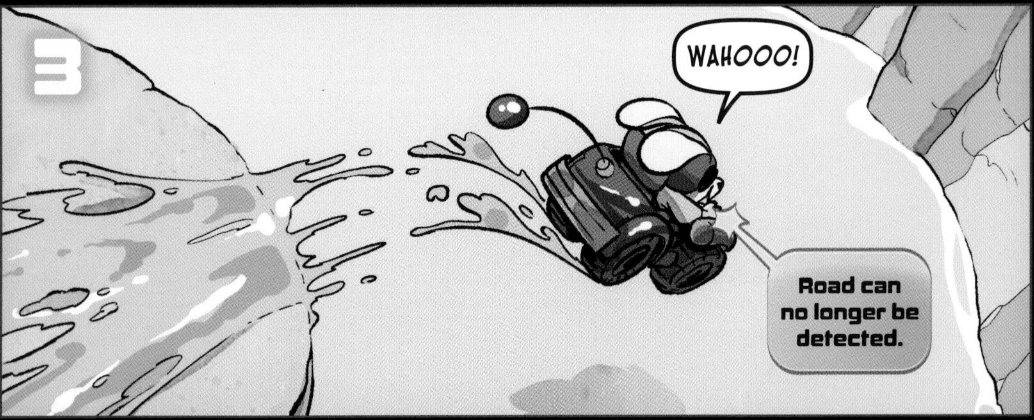
3
WAHOOO!
Road can no longer be detected.

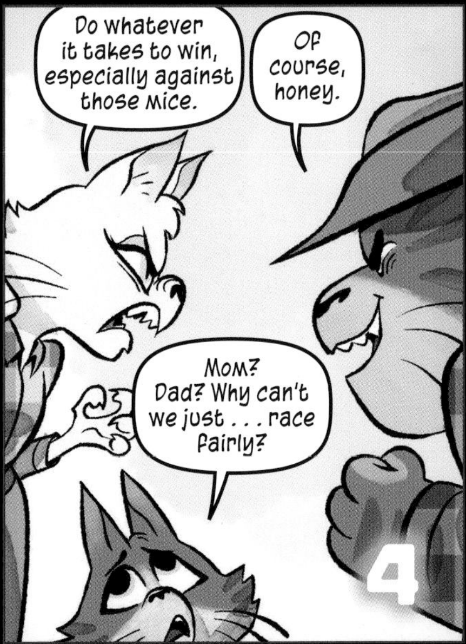
Do whatever it takes to win, especially against those mice.
Of course, honey.
Mom? Dad? Why can't we just . . . race fairly?
4

How do you think Kinny feels about his parents' racing methods? What in the text and art makes you think that?

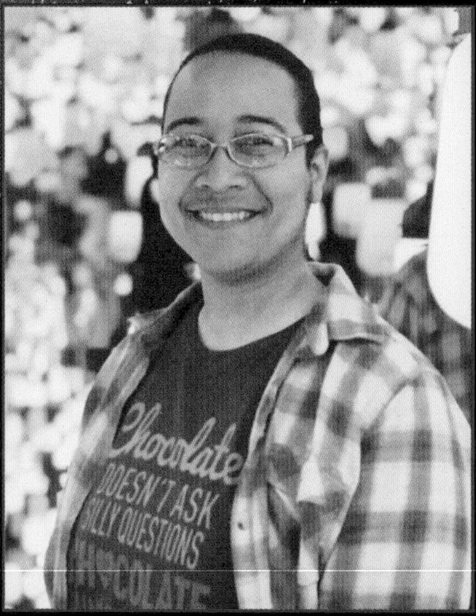
Chocolate
DOESN'T ASK
SILLY QUESTIONS

AUTHOR

Jasmine Walls is a writer, editor, and artist with a passion for fun and inclusive storytelling. She has written comics for all ages with publishers like Levine Querido, Mad Cave Studios, Boom!, and Penguin Random House. She lives in San Diego with her family, two dogs, and a large stash of hot chocolate.

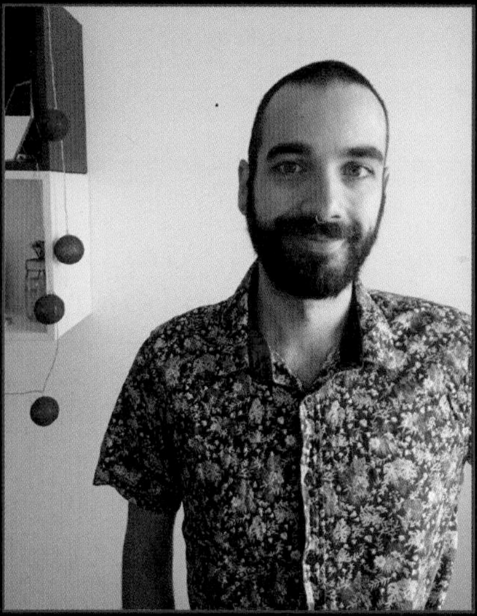

ILLUSTRATOR

Jonatan Cantero is a versatile cartoonist, illustrator, teacher, and art director from Buenos Aires, Argentina. He's been publishing comic books and graphic novels since 1999 in the US, UK, Argentina, Uruguay, France, Spain, and Italy. His work has also appeared in numerous print and digital media, and he's partnered with a variety of publishers around the globe.

GLOSSARY

chalice (CHAL-iss)–a large cup, sometimes used as a trophy

daredevil (DEYR-deh-vuhl)–a person who does dangerous things, especially for attention or because they like the thrill

leg (LEG)–in a relay race, the part of the race done by a single member of the relay team

mod (MOD)–short for modification, a change made to something by the owner in order to make the thing act or look differently

qualify (KWOL-uh-fahy)–to earn a spot in a race based on the times and performance of earlier races

revenge (rih-VENJ)–action taken in return for an injury or offense

rookie (ROOK-ee)–a person who has just started an activity and has little experience

schemer (SKEE-mer)–a person who makes plans to get what they want, often in a dishonest way

sonar (SOH-nar)–a device that measures the distance to an object by bouncing sound waves off the object and timing how long it takes for the waves to return

upgrade (UP-greyd)–to make something better

visuals (VIZH-oo-uhls)–things you look at, such as video, photos, and images, in order to better understand something

AWESOMELY EVER AFTER.

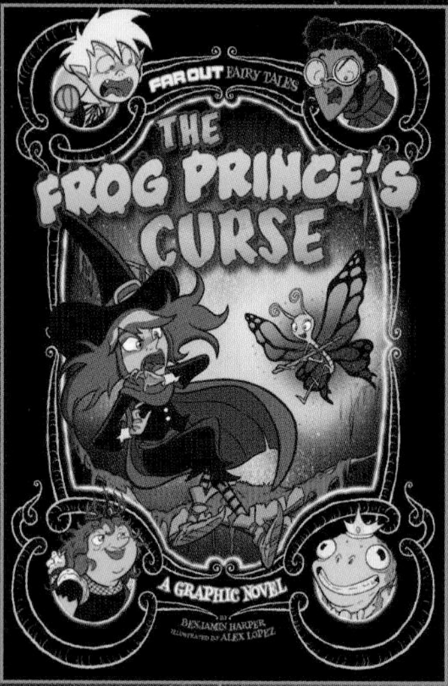
FAR OUT FAIRY TALES
THE FROG PRINCE'S CURSE
A GRAPHIC NOVEL
BENJAMIN HARPER
ALEX LOPEZ

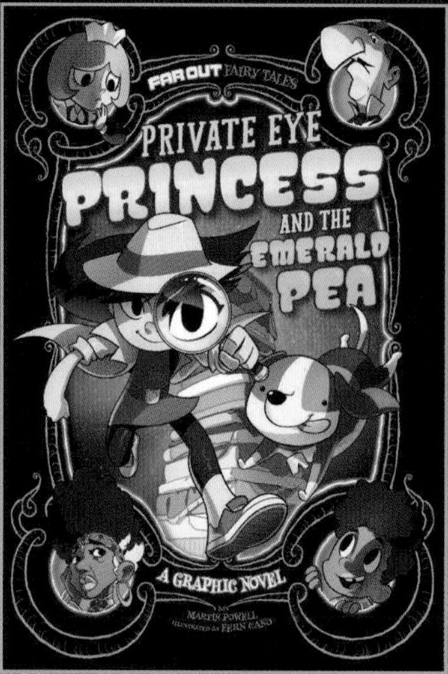
FAR OUT FAIRY TALES
PRIVATE EYE PRINCESS AND THE EMERALD PEA
A GRAPHIC NOVEL
MARTIN POWELL
FERN CANO

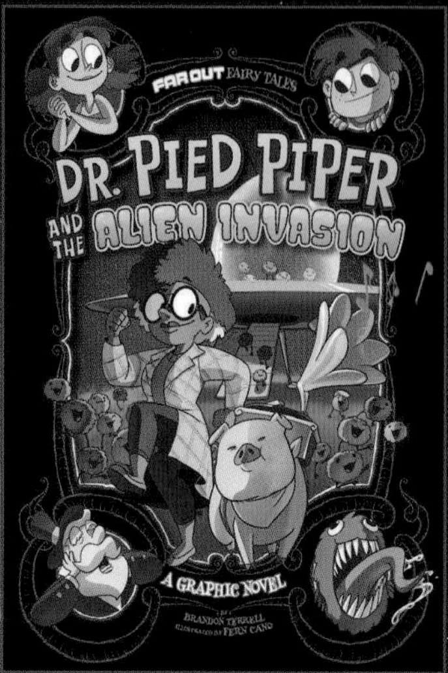
FAR OUT FAIRY TALES
DR. PIED PIPER AND THE ALIEN INVASION
A GRAPHIC NOVEL
BRANDON TERRELL
FERN CANO

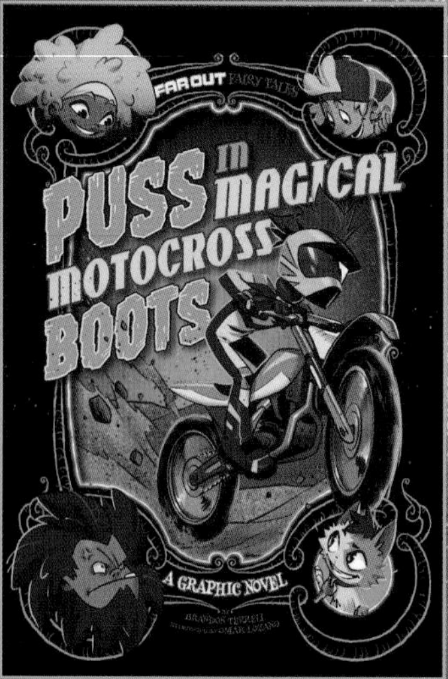
FAR OUT FAIRY TALES
PUSS IN MAGICAL MOTOCROSS BOOTS
A GRAPHIC NOVEL
BRANDON TERRELL
OMAR LOZANO

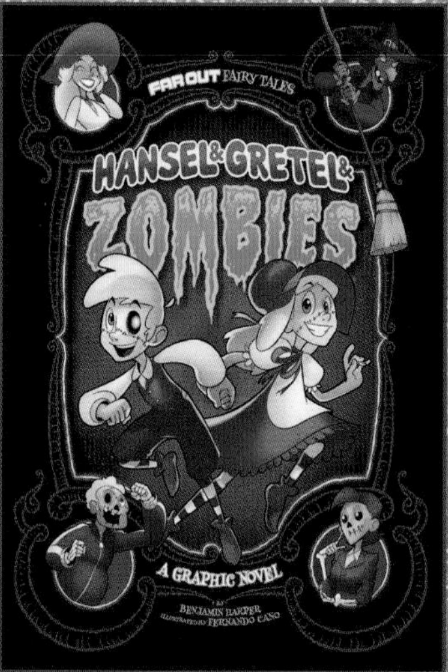
FAR OUT FAIRY TALES
HANSEL & GRETEL & ZOMBIES
A GRAPHIC NOVEL
BENJAMIN HARPER
FERNANDO CANO

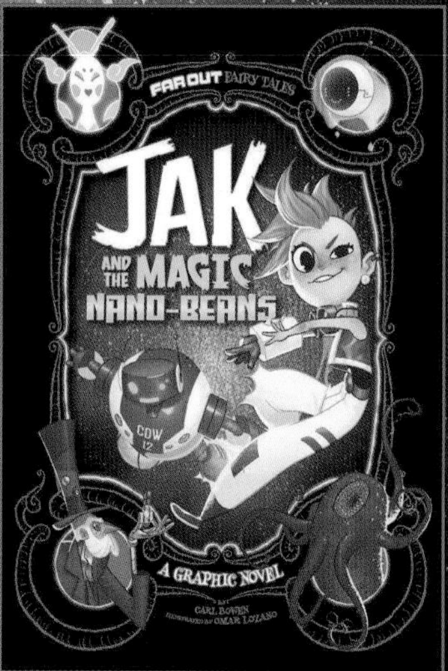
FAR OUT FAIRY TALES
JAK AND THE MAGIC NANO-BEANS
A GRAPHIC NOVEL
CARL BOWEN
OMAR LOZANO

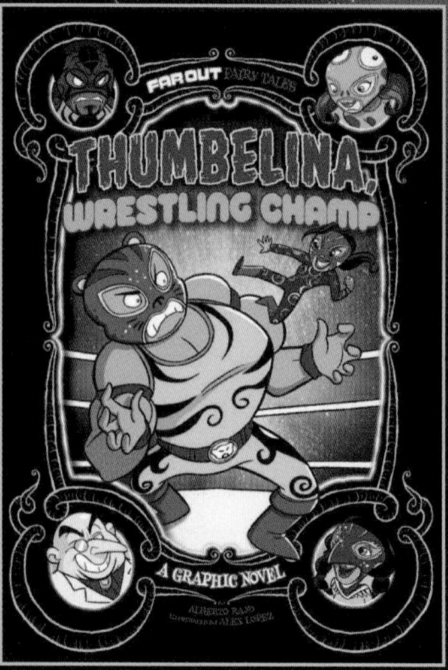
FAR OUT FAIRY TALES
THUMBELINA, WRESTLING CHAMP
A GRAPHIC NOVEL
ALBERTO RAYO
ALEX LOPEZ

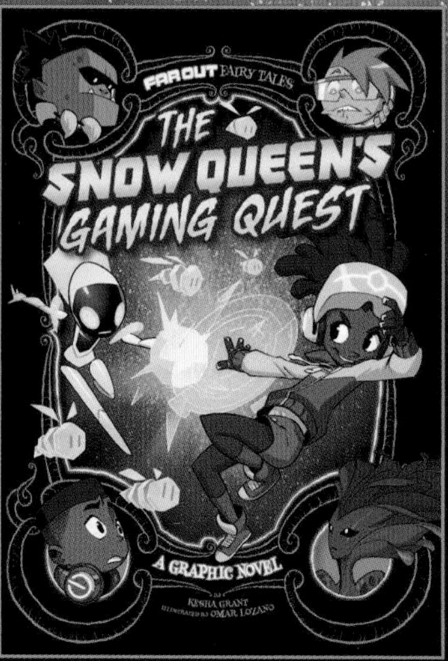
FAR OUT FAIRY TALES
THE SNOW QUEEN'S GAMING QUEST
A GRAPHIC NOVEL
KESHA GRANT
OMAR LOZANO

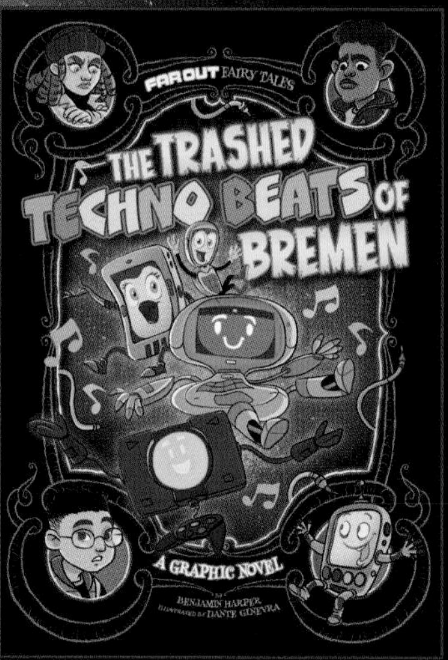
FAR OUT FAIRY TALES
THE TRASHED TECHNO BEATS OF BREMEN
A GRAPHIC NOVEL
BENJAMIN HARPER
DANTE GINEVRA

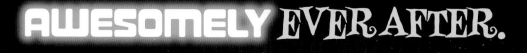